The Third Truth

Also by Michael Bar-Zohar

The Hunt for German Scientists

Ben-Gurion: The Armed Prophet

The Avengers

*Embassies in Crisis: Diplomats and
Demagogues Behind the Six Day War*

*Spies in the Promised Land: Iser Harel
and the Israeli Secret Service*

MICHAEL BAR-ZOHAR

The Third Truth

HOUGHTON MIFFLIN COMPANY BOSTON

1973

FIRST PRINTING V

First American Edition
Copyright © 1973 by Michael Bar-Zohar
All rights reserved. No part of this work may be
reproduced or transmitted in any form by any means,
electronic or mechanical, including photocopying and
recording, or by any information storage or
retrieval system, without permission in
writing from the publisher.

Originally published in French under the title
La Troisième Vérité. © Librairie Arthème Fayard 1972.
Translated into English by June P. Wilson and Walter B. Michaels

PRINTED IN THE UNITED STATES OF AMERICA

Library of Congress Cataloging in Publication Data

Bar-Zohar, Michael.
  The third truth.

  Translation of La troisième vérité.
  I.Title.
PZ4.B2255Th [PQ2662.A75]   843'.9'14   73–5833
ISBN 0–395–15458–8

The Third Truth

1

THE MINISTER'S BODY WAS DISCOVERED ON AUGUST 25TH AT 3.47 a.m. by Sergeant Alan Dudley of the Port Authority police on a routine night patrol of the Lincoln Tunnel. As he was making a turn on the ramp leading into the New Jersey end of the tunnel, Dudley noticed a large gash in the guard rail by the side of the road. The rail had been sliced as if by a saw just where it was riveted to a post. Twisted and battered, it hung from the next post, leaving an opening about six feet wide—just enough for a large car to pass through.

Dudley gave his partner, Sergeant Bruce Flanagan, a dig in the ribs: "Hey, Bruce, what do you make of that?"

The big Irishman had been dozing. He shook himself awake. "What's eating you, pal?" Rubbing his eyes, he leaned forward. "What d'you know ... it looks brand new. Want to bet we find a car down at the bottom?"

Sure enough, there was a wreck on Boulevard East, a good hundred feet below the road. By some miracle it had not caught fire in its plunge down the slope and had come to rest right side up. The first thing Dudley noticed when he reached the car were its licence plates.

"Diplomatic plates," he said as he ran his flashlight over the twisted mass of metal.

The car was a Lincoln Continental and the driver's body was pinned between the steering wheel and the seat. The man was unrecognisable, his face slashed by splinters from the shattered windshield. There was a pool of blood on the

5

leather seat and another on the light grey rug that covered the floor. He was wearing a dark blue suit, silk shirt and dark tie, and near him on the floor lay a thin briefcase of supple black leather. Leaning down, Dudley produced a black chauffeur's cap from under the seat. In the lining was some writing in a foreign script.

"Looks like Russian to me," Flanagan said.

"Russian? You think maybe it's the Ambassador's chauffeur?" Dudley started to look around in the back seat. Suddenly, he straightened up.

"Hey, Bruce, what do you make of this?"

He handed him another hat, a snap brim of excellent quality in a soft dark felt. "Aha! The plot thickens. A two-headed corpse! But where's the other one?"

"Very funny," Dudley grumbled and returned to his search behind the front seat.

"We'll get to the bottom of this yet. It can't be all that complicated." Flanagan walked around the car and slipped one arm through the door as he trained his flashlight on the body with the other. He removed the contents of the dead man's breast pocket and started leafing through them. He stopped suddenly.

"What's the matter? Found something?"

"It's a diplomatic passport!" Flanagan said, his voice rising. "Alan, climb back up to the car and call headquarters. Tell them we've just found the body of the Soviet Foreign Minister. Tell them he died in a car accident."

"The Russian Foreign Minister? You're sure? What's the guy's name . . . Ponomarev?"

"That's the one. Now get going!"

It was a steep climb. Winded and sweating, Dudley got into the police car and called for reinforcements.

Within minutes, three more police cars were on the scene. But it wasn't until an hour later, in the grey light of dawn, that the investigators found two little holes in the dead man's chest. Ponomarev had been killed by two bullets, one of which had gone straight to his heart.

He had been dead before the car ever left the road.

Stanley Hobbs, the Secretary of State, personally called

6

Dimitri Gaidukov, the Soviet Ambassador to the United Nations, to break the news. It was five in the morning. Gaidukov awoke with a start when he heard the phone ring in his Park Avenue apartment. At first, he couldn't make out what the voice at the other end was trying to tell him. Still foggy with sleep, he held the receiver to his ear with one hand while the other groped in the dark for the light switch. Stanley Hobbs had to repeat his carefully rehearsed words several times before the Ambassador finally realised what had happened.

"Assassinated? You're positive? *Assassinated?*" Gaidukov's fingers raked through his white hair.

"Yes, Mr. Ambassador. Unfortunately, it's beyond the shadow of a doubt. The men we've put in charge are absolutely certain. Believe me, we're shocked too. As yet we have no idea how it could have happened. But rest assured, Mr. Ambassador, we will spare no effort in ..."

"*Assassinated!* The Soviet Foreign Minister assassinated on United States soil! *Do you understand what that means?*" The Ambassador's stupefaction turned to rage. "This despicable political assassination may have incalculable consequences. You ... you ..."

Hobbs's voice betrayed his embarrassment and confusion. "Mr. Gaidukov, please do not jump to hasty conclusions. I am every bit as outraged as you are. It's a disaster for the entire world, for the United States as well as the Soviet Union." Then, after a brief hesitation, he added: "I am speaking to you from the White House, and the President ... the President of the United States would like to speak with you."

The familiar voice came on at the other end, but this time, the usual assurance had given way to deep anxiety. "Mr. Ambassador, may I offer my most sincere condolences. I have already dictated a cable to the President of the Council of Ministers, Mr. Kuznietzov, but I wanted to speak with you first. This is a terrible disaster for both our countries. Please believe me when I say that we will do everything in our power to find those responsible for this frightful crime. The Secretary of State is leaving by special plane immediately in order to see you."

7

"This is terrible! Terrible. Terrible!" Gaidukov kept repeating the word like an automaton.

"I understand only too well what you are feeling," the President continued. "I too am appalled. And I promise you as President of the United States, as a friend, and as a man who sincerely aspires to strengthen the bonds between our two countries, that we will spare no effort to discover the authors of this monstrous crime. I ask only that you and the personnel of the Soviet delegation to the U.N. give all the help you can to the security officers we will put in charge of the investigation."

The President's voice grew indistinct for a moment and Gaidukov caught snatches of a muffled conversation.

"Please forgive the interruption, Mr. Ambassador, but I've just been informed that, in accordance with my instructions, a special group of investigators has already been assembled which includes the top agents of the F.B.I. and the best experts in the New York City police force. I have also asked the Secretary of State to deliver a personal letter of condolence to Mrs. Ponomarev. The unfortunate death of the Soviet Foreign Minister is a heavy blow to relations between our two countries. But I am certain, Mr. Ambassador, and I have stated it also in my message to President Kuznietzov, that our joint efforts will make it possible to resolve this crisis. Thank you, Mr. Ambassador, and goodbye. And may I say again that I fully understand the significance of this disaster."

Still feeling the buffeting effects of the shock, Gaidukov slowly shook his head and said into the now disconnected phone: "No, Mr. President, for all your good intentions, you do not understand its full significance at all."

BASE IMPERIALIST PLOT was *Pravda*'s front page headline. The article itself, unsigned, accused "Wall Street magnates, the fascist right wing, and warmongers of the United States", and violently attacked the American administration for not providing sufficient protection for the Soviet Foreign Minister. It went on: "We accuse the United States of planting a knife in our back on the eve of the Zurich Disarmament

8

Conference ... Those who are responsible, on every level, must be punished ..."

Izvestia reported an extraordinary session of the Politburo and an emergency meeting of the Central Committee of the Communist Party. "This abject assassination is consistent with the bloodthirsty tradition of the forces of world reaction who will stop at nothing to impede the forward march of the forces of progress and freedom ..."

The *Red Flag*, official organ of the Soviet Army was the most virulent. Under the heading SACRIFICED TO MOLOCH, editor-in-chief Sergei Lavrentiev, proclaimed: "Comrade Lev Ponomarev is the victim of an unspeakable plot. Imperialist agents and C.I.A. mercenaries murdered the U.S.S.R. representative to the family of nations in cold blood ... The government of the U.S.S.R. must immediately break off diplomatic relations with this gang of assassins ... All further meetings with representatives of rampant imperialism and the almighty dollar must henceforth be rejected. We will not take part in the Zurich Conference!"

Radio Peking, quoting the editorial in the *People's Daily*, proclaimed: "The assassination of Minister Ponomarev is the fruit of a vile plot hatched in concert by Washington imperialists and Moscow revisionists. The governments of the United States and the U.S.S.R. made common cause in order to rid themselves of that valiant fighter for justice, equality and socialism—Comrade Ponomarev. His death leaves the way clear for that pack of reactionary dogs in Moscow and Washington who dream of a criminal assault on China. But this assault by the paper tigers will flounder against the forces of progress united under our Chairman, Mao Tse-Tung."

A wave of anti-American demonstrations swept through the capitals of the world. In Moscow, thousands of workers filed silently past the American Embassy as mounted police prevented any eruption of violence. But in Cairo, Damascus, and Amman, frenzied crowds, obeying an ancient tradition, burned down the American cultural centres. In Budapest, Prague and Sophia, demonstrators stoned the American Embassies. American tourists were mauled in Chili and in Guinea. In Brazil, the American Ambassador narrowly escaped a kidnapping attempt. In Peking, a mob of Red Guards attacked the British Consul, holding him captive in his car for four hours while they shouted insults, shook their fists and brandished Mao's Little Red Book. Paris, Bonn and Stockholm were also the scene of stormy demonstrations organised by elements of the extreme left, for the most part Maoists.

"The assassination of Lev Ponomarev threatens to have serious political consequences," wrote the chief editorial writer for the London *Times*. "Ponomarev represented the hard-line Stalinists and chiefs of the Red Army. Thanks to the Army's support, he enjoyed a privileged position at the centre of the Soviet government which dared not limit his powers. In the West, he was considered one of the leading opponents of the Zurich Disarmament Conference, and was suspected of working with elements in Communist China in order to create a common front against the United States. His sudden death raises many questions and threatens to increase the military pressure on the Kremlin to cancel the Zurich Conference."

Le Monde was oracular: "The mysterious death of the only member of the Soviet government who might have wished to torpedo the Zurich Conference and end the rapprochement between the U.S. and the U.S.S.R. is indeed subject for reflection. Although political assassination has gone out of fashion in the free world, we must not overlook the fact that the sudden disappearance of the leading Soviet diplomat is very convenient for the White House, and even, to a large extent, for the Kremlin 'troika' ... The accusations made by the *People's Daily* in Peking hinting at a plot between certain groups in Russia and America to eliminate Ponomarev, may seem fantastic on first reading; but on further reflection, we must admit they are not without logic."

The American press was unanimous in its expressions of deep concern, and its demand for a speedy and thorough investigation. With the exception of the *Southern Star and Herald*, which was overjoyed at "the disappearance of that sworn enemy of the United States", the American papers hoped that the killers would be quickly found and that the murder would not harm relations between the U.S. and the

U.S.S.R. "Mr. Ponomarev was a declared enemy of the United States and this very fact makes it urgent that his murder be cleared up as soon as possible," editorialised the *New York Times*. "The people of both the United States and the Soviet Union have placed their hopes on a rapprochement between the two great powers. To this end, the Zurich Conference is of extreme importance, and only a quick solution to the mystery can save it."

N.B.C. commentator, George Skidmore, stated before the television cameras: "With Ponomarev's death, there is a strong possibility that Dimitri Gaidukov will be named Foreign Minister. Mr. Gaidukov, who represents his country on the Security Council of the U.N., is known for his moderate position and is considered a strong partisan of rapprochement between Moscow and Washington."

Dimitri Gaidukov took off his thick tortoise-shell glasses and rubbed his eyes with the palms of his hands. He hadn't had a minute's rest for the past twenty-four hours. The offices of the Soviet delegation to the U.N. were in an uproar. The continuous round of condolences, reporters' telephone calls, U.S. officials and foreign diplomats, as well as the predictable anonymous threats, had exhausted him. There had been a battery of cables and telephone conversations with Moscow and here was yet another cable just placed on his desk. Typed on a piece of thin white paper with two diagonal red lines, it was marked "Ultra secret: Personal". The telegram was signed "Yakovlev", an alias for Gregory Efremenko, chief of K.G.B., the Soviet Secret Service. Gaidukov rarely exchanged telegrams with Efremenko. He had no desire to. Secret affairs were the domain of Anatoli Serafimov who was attached to the delegation as the "representative of the Academy of Soviet Science to the U.N. Scientific Commission". In fact, Serafimov was the personal representative of the head of Soviet intelligence for all of North America. A tall man, dry and close-mouthed, he was made to order for his post. With his innocuous appearance, he moved about unnoticed. Moreover, since his scientific knowledge and titles were authentic, his "cover" was impeccable.

Serafimov waited patiently while Gaidukov read the telegram. When he had finished, he wiped his brow, propped his chin on his fists and contemplated the telegram. Without looking up, he said: "I have to admit that this is absolutely astounding."

Serafimov was silent.

"Complete co-operation," Gaidukov muttered, throwing a glance at the secret agent. "Look, there it is, in black and white!" And he jabbed at each word with his stubby finger: "'We request that you co-operate completely with the American Secret Service and that you provide them with every possible assistance.' Anatoli Ilitch, your friends astonish me. The chief of K.G.B. orders me to reveal all the delegation's secrets to the Americans. It's ... it's nothing short of incredible!"

"Excuse me, Comrade Gaidukov, but read what follows: 'These instructions do not apply to the current business of the delegation, its activities or its documents. You must continue to protect these with the utmost vigilance.' That means that ..."

"I know, I know." Gaidukov gestured impatiently. "I can read too. But whether we like it or not, this telegram means that I must open the delegation's door to American agents, allow them to interrogate our personnel on how we function, even on the personal habits and intimate friends of the dead Minister and the members of the delegation."

"Put simply, it means that Moscow has decided to comply with White House demands and to collaborate with the American authorities."

Gaidukov was silent for a moment. "Strange. Very strange. Frankly, after the furious reaction in Moscow I was all ready to pack my bags. Instead, I'm ordered to admit American secret agents into the delegation!"

"Your conclusions, Comrade Gaidukov, were ... how shall I say ... somewhat premature. Only the *Red Flag* asked for your recall or openly accused the American administration. In point of fact, *Pravda* and *Izvestia* were quite cautious."

Gaidukov was thoughtful. "Yes, they do seem to attach great importance to the Zurich Conference." Then he rose abruptly from his chair. "So, what do you want of me? Are they already here?"

"Yes, they have just arrived. Bill Pattison from the F.B.I., an officer of the New York police named Rogers, and a young liaison man from the State Department."

"Have you talked with them?"

For the first time, the shadow of a smile passed over Serafimov's face. "Certainly not! They barely know I exist. The only one who has seen them is our security officer, Shuvakin. He's our delegation official representative in this affair."

"All right. Show them in," Gaidukov grumbled as he pressed the button on his intercom.

Serafimov left the Ambassador's office but halted behind the door just long enough to hear Gaidukov's deep voice say in English: "Come in, gentlemen, come in. Mr. Shuvakin, our security officer, and I will do everything in our power to help your investigation. Both my government and I personally..." Serafimov smiled as he left delegation headquarters.

The thunderstorm was reaching its climax as the blue Toronado pulled up to the curb on East 50th Street. The rain was coming down in sheets, drenching the three men who leapt from the car and ran for shelter under the marquee of the Waldorf Towers. It was only five in the afternoon but the sombre clouds over the city had plunged it into premature night.

As the three men entered the lobby, a young man in a grey suit picked up the house phone.

"They're here, sir."

"Send them right up. The Secretary is waiting."

Stanley Hobbs was pacing back and forth across the spacious drawing room of his eighteenth-floor suite. It included a bedroom, two rooms where his assistants worked during the day, and an office with a panoramic view, furnished with two tables and a battery of deep leather chairs. The Secretary's friends were fond of saying that nothing stimulated this son of a New England village like the view of the bustling city at his feet. But on this occasion, neither the city panorama nor the frequent telephone calls from his assistants in Washington were able to relieve his tension.

Every fifteen minutes, he was on the phone to his liaison man at New York police headquarters to find out if anything had turned up. A car had been waiting since noon at the U.S.S.R. delegation to pick up the three investigators the moment they emerged.

Bill Pattison entered the room first. He was a small man whose head jutted forward from his thick neck. This, together with his underslung jaw and stubborn expression, suggested a bulldog. He was in fact one of the best investigators in the F.B.I. Among his biggest successes were several spectacular exploits against the Mafia when Robert Kennedy was Attorney-General.

Now, however, he seemed ill at ease, shifting from one foot to the other. "Sir, for the moment, I'm afraid we have nothing to report."

Hobbs invited the men to sit down. Rogers, the police officer, had followed Pattison in and now sat on the edge of a chair. The young man from the State Department leaned against the wall, melting into the decor in a manner befitting a well-trained State Department underling.

"All the same, I'd like some sort of preliminary report," Hobbs said, lighting a cigarette and throwing the match into a large brass ashtray already overflowing with stubs. "Call them your first impressions, if you like."

Pattison pulled two notebooks from his breast pocket and started to leaf through them. "O.K. You know the beginning. The car, the body ... The autopsy established the time of death at around a half-hour before the body was discovered. Death was instantaneous: two bullets shot from a distance of between a hundred and a hundred and fifty feet." He looked up at the Secretary. "We can tell this from the bullets' force of impact. The weapon used was a carbine—a .32 calibre Winchester Special. I'd like to point out that this particular gun can be used with a very precise telescopic lens. The killer was a real virtuoso. The two bullets were fired one right after the other. They went through the windshield and struck Minister Ponomarev in the chest." Pattison was silent for a moment. "Sir, I want to emphasise that the killer was an exceptional marksman. You could count on the fingers of one hand the number of men in the American Army who could

14

do as well. And in the middle of the night."

"Have you any idea how the murder was set up?"

"Only hypotheses, sir. From what we know so far, there appear to have been at least two people involved: the killer and his accomplice—who did the driving. We think they parked on a local road near the top of the escarpment that overlooks the ramp. The killer stationed himself on the retaining wall above the road and waited for the car to come into his line of fire as it slowed down on the curve. We found footprints up there between the local road and the wall. Because of the dark, the killer could not have identified the driver although he knew the car." Pattison warmed to his subject. "The Minister's car comes along. The killer is already aiming in his direction. The Lincoln comes within range and he shoots twice. The car swerves to the right, snaps the guard rail and crashes down the slope."

The Secretary stopped him. "Wait a minute. That means the car wasn't coming from New York."

"That's right, sir. The car was going from New Jersey to New York."

Hobbs leapt from his chair. "Can you tell me what the Soviet Foreign Minister was doing alone, in New Jersey, in the middle of the night, and why the devil he was on his way back to New York at three in the morning?"

Pattison exchanged a brief glance with Rogers. His voice betrayed his embarrassment. "Well, sir, that's the problem. Right now, we just don't know."

"What about the delegation? Couldn't they help you?"

"So far as I could tell, they did everything they could. They let us question anybody we wanted. Of course, their security officer, Shuvakin, tagged after us the whole time, but I didn't feel they were trying to hide anything from us. I think they're just as concerned as we are."

Rogers broke in: "Bill, why don't you reconstruct the Minister's movements before the crime for Mr. Hobbs?"

"Would that interest you, sir?" Pattison examined his notebook again.

"It certainly would. I'd like to know everything the Minister did from the moment he set foot in the United States."

"Well, let's see: he arrived in New York two days before the murder, in other words, the day before yesterday. He had just spent a week in Cuba, on an official visit. In New York, as usual, he stayed at the Plaza. He didn't leave his room that afternoon. Ambassador Gaidukov joined him there and they discussed current problems due to come before the U.N. General Assembly. That night, he gave a dinner in honour of the Ambassadors from Hungary, Poland and Bulgaria. It must have been a spur of the moment thing, because the other Ambassadors from the Eastern Europe bloc—Czechoslovakia and Rumania—weren't even in New York. The guests left around eleven and he returned to his room. His bodyguard and two secretaries spent the night in near-by rooms.

"On the day of the murder, the Minister spent most of the morning at the Soviet delegation offices on First Avenue. A little before noon, he paid an official call on the Secretary-General. He had lunch with Ambassador Gaidukov and returned to delegation headquarters. He stayed there until four thirty. Then he returned to the Plaza, but promised Gaidukov that he would be back at seven p.m. for a reception in honour of the President of Egypt." Pattison opened his second notebook. "All right. At six fifteen, he telephoned Gaidukov to say he couldn't make the reception and asked him to offer his excuses to the Egyptians. He gave no reason. The delegation assures us that there was no political motive behind the change in plans. The Minister also asked Gaidukov to have his chauffeur, Arkadi Slobodin, get in touch with him. Slobodin had been his chauffeur for two years in Moscow before he was transferred to New York a year ago. Whenever the Minister came to New York, he used Slobodin as his personal chauffeur. The Ambassador would put his official car at Ponomarev's disposal and use another car belonging to the delegation.

"It was six fifty and the reception was already underway when Slobodin asked the Ambassador if he would need the car that evening because the Minister wanted it. Naturally, the Ambassador made no objection. Slobodin was told to be at the service entrance of the Plaza at nine thirty—he was there as instructed. The Minister appeared on time without his bodyguard and told Slobodin to go home; he would drive himself. Slobodin gave him the keys to the car and took the subway home."

"Didn't that surprise Slobodin? The Minister asking to drive the car himself?" Hobbs got up from his chair and lit another cigarette. "Did Ponomarev know New York and the suburbs that well?"

Pattison shrugged. "Slobodin told us that this wasn't the first time the Minister had taken the car alone. And you have to remember that Ponomarev was Ambassador to Washington for three years and naturally spent a good deal of time in New York."

"Yes, yes, of course. But doesn't Slobodin have any idea where the Minister was going?"

"None. At least, that's what he says. He was the last person to see the Minister alive. Ponomarev left the hotel at nine thirty and was found dead six hours later. What happened between is a thick fog."

Hobbs was about to get up when Rogers leaned forward to catch his attention.

"You have something to add?" Hobbs asked.

"I don't know what bearing it has on the murder, Mr. Secretary"—Rogers spoke with great deference—"but Bill and I were both struck by one particular point: there seems to have been no reason for the Minister to be in New York in the first place."

"What do you mean?" Hobbs shot back. "We were informed that the Minister would be coming to New York on a private visit before returning to Moscow."

"Yes, I know. Ambassador Gaidukov was also advised of the visit. But he acknowledged that it was nothing more than a stop-over and that there was nothing going on that required the Minister's presence. He could have gone straight to Moscow from Cuba. Gaidukov thinks he might have wanted to talk with the delegation here to prepare himself for the Zurich Conference. But there was nothing concrete, nothing urgent."

Hobbs gave him a long look. "Maybe you've got something there; maybe that's all it was—an ordinary routine visit, a chance to stop by for a few days, something like that . . .

Tell me, did you also have the impression the Russians are being above-board? What I mean is..."

There was a discreet ring from the telephone on the Secretary's desk. He picked up the receiver.

"It's for you," and he handed the receiver to Pattison. "It's from headquarters."

The F.B.I. agent listened for several minutes then placed his hand over the mouthpiece and turned towards the Secretary of State. "This is a little unexpected, sir. They've just received a call from Slobodin. He wants to see either Rogers or me. He says it's important and wants the conversation strictly private. Is it all right if I accept?"

Hobbs started. "What do you mean, private? Without Shuvakin's knowledge? Without the Russians'?"

"That's what they're saying, sir. They also say that Slobodin seems very agitated. They have him on another line. They were able to trace the call to a phone booth in the Howard Johnson's at the corner of Broadway and 47th."

"O.K. Go ahead," Hobbs said. "Accept, but not today. Make the meeting for tomorrow morning. Maybe we can find out first why he is scared of Shuvakin."

"Right," Pattison said into the receiver. "Say I'll meet him tomorrow at eight sharp ... in the coffee shop opposite track 13 in Grand Central Station. It's quiet then and we can talk unobserved."

But the meeting with Slobodin never took place. Not long after midnight, the building superintendent discovered Arkadi Slobodin lying across the entrance of his apartment house at 77 East 16th Street. He had been shot by two bullets from a .32 calibre Winchester Special.

2

TANIA SLOBODIN WAS DRY-EYED. A SMALL MATERNAL-LOOKING woman around forty, she had on a black dress, a heavy wool sweater and plain, sturdy shoes. Her head was covered by a brown scarf from which a few strands of black hair protruded. She sat calmly in her chair, her hands folded in her lap. She had passed beyond tears or rage and seemed enveloped in the kind of apathy that follows major disasters.

Shuvakin and Pattison sat opposite her without speaking. Pattison was exhausted. Since the telephone call had awakened him at five o'clock in the morning, the hours had clicked by in a demented rhythm: telephone calls to the Secretary of State, to the chief of the F.B.I., to Shuvakin, the dramatic interview with Ambassador Gaidukov, the rush to the police laboratory, the examination of the murder site, the desperate effort to convince the New York police not to inform the press. He was now feeling the effects, sitting in this shabby little apartment across from the Russian woman in mourning to whom all he could think to say was: "I am responsible for your husband's death", or "If I had agreed to see him last night, he might still be alive". But he kept silent, stealing an occasional glance at Shuvakin whose face remained a blank.

It was Tania Slobodin who spoke first. She said something in Russian to Shuvakin who then turned to Pattison. "Her English is poor. She would like to speak in Russian and I'll translate."

Pattison nodded his agreement.

She spoke a few sentences without a trace of emotion. Shuvakin translated: "She says you should ask yourself why her husband wanted to talk to you alone, without my knowledge."

Pattison could not conceal his unease. "It's all right," Shuvakin said, "these things happen. Perhaps he had good reasons. In any event, it was she who advised him to go to see you when she saw how he was torturing himself, regretting he hadn't told you everything he knew. But first she wants to know how he was killed. So far, no one has been willing to tell her and I myself don't know all the details."

These last words were said in a tone of reproach but Pattison decided to overlook it. "In fact, I've only just received the complete report. Apparently the murderers were the same people who killed the Minister. The ballistics lab has established this beyond question."

Shuvakin translated quickly. The chauffeur's widow listened with no visible emotion.

"As opposed to the murder of the Foreign Minister, which was committed in an isolated spot with a minimum of risks, it looks as if Slobodin's killers acted in extreme haste. The first murder appeared to be carefully thought out, whereas Slobodin's seemed improvised. It was a miracle they weren't caught. The killer stationed himself on the second floor of the building across the street, near the window on the staircase landing. We established this fact from the bullet's angle of impact. As Slobodin crossed the sidewalk to enter his building, the killer shot twice, and ran down the stairs into a waiting automobile. We interrogated the tenants of the building. Most of them say they heard the shots but paid no attention or thought it was the exhaust from a car or motorcycle. A few of them admitted they knew it must be gun shots but they were afraid to go out. You know how people are these days in New York—afraid to get involved. In any case, two of them called the police. A tenant on the sixth floor whose apartment faces the street said that he noticed someone run out of the house right after the shots and disappear into a car which immediately set off. Because of the distance and the dark, he couldn't make out how

20

many people were in the car or what the licence number was. All he remembered was that it was a big dark-coloured car, that its motor was running and its headlights turned off.

"We set up road blocks at every tunnel and bridge but the killers must have gotten away in the first fifteen minutes after the murder. We're now checking every police file in the country to see if there's any record on the rifle. By comparing bullets from the .32 calibre Winchester we might be able to identify the rifle and even the owner. Of course, the rifle would have had to be used in a previous crime and the owner identified at that time. But the chances for that are practically zero."

The widow asked a brief question.

Shuvakin translated: "Did he suffer greatly?"

Pattison looked at her. She hadn't moved. Only her eyes were now looking down and he noticed a slight trembling of her hands.

"No," he said. "He didn't suffer at all. His death was instantaneous."

For several minutes there was a heavy silence. Pattison couldn't bring himself to ask the question on the tip of his tongue. He didn't want it to look as if he were trying to bargain with her: I tell you how your husband died; you tell me what I want to know...

Once again it was Tania Slobodin who spoke first.

"She says that her husband knew where the Minister went before the assassination."

Pattison sat up.

"She says he didn't want to tell you at the time of the interrogation. Her husband was very attached to the Minister. He had served under him in the Second World War when Ponomarev was a colonel in the Second Byelorussian Division which was surrounded and captured near Kiev. Ponomarev managed to escape with a handful of soldiers and won the Red Star for it. Slobodin was in the group that held the Germans off until Ponomarev and his men made their escape. He was taken prisoner and moved from one prisoner-of-war camp to another, finally ending up at Dachau in Germany."

"At Dachau?" Pattison was surprised. "I didn't know there

21

were Russian prisoners-of-war at Dachau. I thought there were only Jews."

"No. It's not generally known, but there were Russian prisoners too. And when Slobodin returned to Russia after the war, he was treated like a leper, as were all the other repatriated prisoners. As you probably know, during the Stalin period, any Russian who allowed himself to be taken prisoner was considered a traitor. It was at that point that Ponomarev, who was rising high in the Party, intervened on Slobodin's behalf and saw to his rehabilitation. He took him on as chauffeur and they became close friends. Slobodin's admiration for him was boundless. He would have done anything for him."

"Then why didn't he speak up yesterday?"

Shuvakin looked uncomfortable. "He probably didn't want to damage his reputation."

Pattison looked straight at the Russian. "Are you trying to tell me that Ponomarev did something dishonest or shameful that night?"

"No," Shuvakin said. "Not shameful really. A weakness, perhaps. A simple weakness. After all, he was human like the rest of us. And apparently Slobodin realised I hadn't mentioned it to you and therefore he didn't say anything either."

Pattison felt his anger rise.

"You *both* knew? You knew and told me nothing? And that's what you call 'complete co-operation'? You're playing a double game, a dirty hypocritical game..."

"This is no time for insults, Mr. Pattison." Shuvakin was so obviously upset that Pattison calmed down. "I said nothing because I didn't see how it could have any bearing on the murder. Slobodin felt differently. He wanted to tell you because he thought it might help you find the killers."

"All right then. Where did Ponomarev spend the night?"

Shuvakin retreated into his shell. "Tania Slobodin says that her husband knew Ponomarev was going to visit ... well, visit someone who was expecting him."

"Who was this someone?" It was a battle to get anything out of this close-lipped Russian.

"A woman."

"What!" Pattison flushed. "A woman? Here, in America?"

22

Shuvakin nodded. "He had a woman friend here. A Russian who . . . who lives here."

"Who is this woman?" This time, Pattison looked directly into Tania Slobodin's eyes. *"Koia? Koia jenschtchina?"* he stammered in bad Russian.

Tania spoke a few words to Shuvakin.

"She doesn't know. Only her husband knew. All he told her was that the Minister was visiting a woman."

Pattison was quiet for several minutes, his chin propped on his fists. The two Russians respected his silence. When he finally raised his head, there was a sly look in his eye.

"But you know, don't you?" he said to Shuvakin.

Shuvakin looked at Pattison for a moment, then he rose to his feet, went over to Tania Slobodin, squeezed her hand, and with a gentleness that surprised Pattison, patted her on the shoulder.

He turned to Pattison: "Come. I'll take you to her."

The Toronado hummed through the Lincoln Tunnel with Pattison at the wheel. On the New Jersey side, he noticed workmen repairing a section of the guard rail. A few cars were parked by the side of the road and a group of people were staring at the scene of the crime. Pattison gave a wry smile as he considered the fascination people felt for murder, gore—this obsession that drove them to watch executions, or elbow their way for a better look at the victim of an accident or a murder and gorge themselves on the sight of a bloody corpse.

"Ambassador Gaidukov didn't know," Shuvakin said suddenly.

Until that moment, the Russian hadn't opened his mouth. Before leaving, he had asked Pattison not to bring anyone with him. He had explained the route to take, then lapsed into a frozen silence. Pattison sympathised. He understood that for Shuvakin to have to tell an American secret agent the details of a Soviet leader's private life, to strip a dead man bare, as it were, was like an act of treason. He knew Shuvakin was doing himself violence, so he left him alone. But now the Russian himself had broken the silence.

Pattison asked: "What do you mean?"

"Gaidukov knew nothing about this. About this woman. In fact, nobody at the delegation knew. Except for Slobodin and myself, of course. Slobodin had once driven the Minister to her house and had waited for him the whole night in the car. Ponomarev never asked him again. But whenever he wanted to drive the car alone, Slobodin knew where he was going."

"What about you?"

Shuvakin smiled. "A security officer is supposed to know these things. I was in charge of Ponomarev's security on many occasions. Very discreetly, of course. Slobodin told me. I followed Ponomarev a couple of times until he became aware of it and ordered me to stop. From then on, he went to his rendezvous entirely alone."

"And you never told the Ambassador?" Pattison asked as they turned off on Route 57 to Simpson.

"Of course not. It was none of his business. I only told him this morning after I learned that Slobodin had been assassinated and that he had wanted to speak with you. It was Gaidukov who ordered me to tell you everything. You can imagine that I would never have done it without his command. I would have prevented the wife from talking too. In fact, both women."

Pattison did not ask him how he would have brought this off.

Number 860 Mimosa Drive in Simpson, New Jersey, was identical to hundreds of thousands of suburban houses around New York: two stories, separated from the street by a small lawn. Pattison automatically guessed at its price: around twenty thousand dollars, probably.

"Is the house hers?" he asked Shuvakin.

"No, of course not. It is owned by the Soviet government."

Pattison looked surprised.

"Oh, didn't I tell you...?" Shuvakin said with forced innocence. "Her husband, Dimitri Kirilenko, is the agricultural attaché to our delegation."

He walked up the path to the house ahead of Pattison, climbed the three steps and was about to ring the doorbell when the door opened.

"Good morning, Olga Petrovna."

24

The woman nodded. She wasn't beautiful in the ordinary sense—her mouth was too large, her grey eyes too far apart, her body a little on the heavy side. But there was a kind of pride, something regal in the way she held herself, in her steady gaze, and the way the thick dark hair swayed against her shoulders as she walked. No, Pattison had no trouble at all imagining why Ponomarev was drawn to this house during his nights in New York. A far cry from the pale, plump little wife whose picture he had seen in the papers: not yet forty, and already beginning to look like the classic Russian *babouchka*.

"How do you do," Pattison said, and turning to Shuvakin, he asked: "Does she know who I am?"

"I understand English," she said with a heavy Slavic accent. "I suppose you are a colleague of Sergei Ivanovitch." Shuvakin nodded. "Please come in."

It was less an invitation than a tactical concession. Olga Kirilenko made no move to sit down, nor did she invite her guests to do so.

"I know that this situation must be very painful for you ... and embarrassing..." Pattison was fumbling. "But we have to ask you a few questions. And I guarantee you absolute secrecy."

"What do you want to know?"

"I would like you to tell us about your relations with the Foreign Minister and anything you can about the night of the murder."

She looked at him, then started talking in a voice drained of all emotion, as if she were a robot with a tape-recorder hidden inside.

"I was Lev Ponomarev's private secretary when he was Ambassador to Washington. That is when our liaison began. My husband was a minor official in the Embassy. We returned to Moscow in 1962 and were sent on a mission to the Far East in 1964. Lev and I saw each other only rarely. We were transferred to New York in 1968 when my husband was made the agricultural attaché to the U.N. delegation. Since then, whenever Lev Ponomarev came through New York, we tried to see each other. Usually he came here. My husband is often away; he travels a great deal all over the United

States. Lev Ponomarev was with me the night he was murdered—from ten in the evening until a little after three a.m. Does that satisfy you?"

Pattison felt a little ridiculous in front of this woman who seemed so much in control of the situation. He wasn't directing the interrogation; she was, and saying only what she wanted to say. Tough as nails, he thought to himself, then asked: "Did you notice anything peculiar in the Minister's behaviour that night? What I mean is, did he seem worried about anything ... did he think he was being followed?"

"No."

"Does your husband know about your relations with Ponomarev?"

For the first time, she hesitated. "I don't know. I don't think so. And I don't know what he would have done if he had found out."

"Do you think he could have killed the Minister out of jealousy?"

She showed no change of expression except for a fleeting look of contempt. "No. My husband did not kill Lev Ponomarev."

"Where is your husband now?"

"He left last week to tour the Middle Western corn fields. At the moment, he should be either in Milwaukee or Kansas City. I don't expect him back before next week."

"Did the Minister tell you what brought him to New York?"

"Yes," she said with a hint of pride. "He said he had no reason at all to come to the United States but that he had taken advantage of his trip to Cuba to stop off in New York and see me. He emphasised that he had come only to see me. He said: 'The consultations, the dinners, the official visits to the U.N. are all window-dressing.' I don't think anybody knew. No, to be truthful, I knew that his chauffeur, Slobodin, knew. I also suspected that Sergei Shuvakin knew. Since he was the security officer and had to follow the Minister wherever he went, he had to know. But those are the only two."

"When did you learn he was coming to New York?"

"I knew nothing up to the last minute. The day before

he came, I was invited—along with the other delegation wives—to a party given by Ania Efremova, the wife of Ambassador Gaidukov's right-hand man. It was she who told us that the Minister was arriving the next day on an unofficial visit."

"When he left you that night, did the Minister tell you his plans?"

"All he said was that he was leaving for Moscow the next afternoon."

As Pattison paused for a moment, she broke in: "If you have no further questions, I'd be very grateful if we could stop now. I'd like to be alone."

When the door closed behind them, Pattison thought he heard the sound of muffled sobs.

They were about to get into the car when Pattison said: "I have to get in touch with headquarters. I wonder if..."

Shuvakin understood right away. "I'll stretch my legs for a bit," and he walked away, feigning great interest in the maple trees that lined the street.

Pattison got into the car and called police headquarters. "This is urgent. I want a report on Dimitri Kirilenko, agricultural attaché to the U.N. Soviet delegation. He's now on a visit to the corn belt and should be either in Milwaukee or Kansas City. I want to know everything he's done since he left New York to the present moment. In particular, I want you to find out if he could have left his hotel the night before last, taken a plane to New York and been back by dawn. Same thing for last night. Find out if he could have been in New York around midnight. I also want to know if he has had any dealings with people unrelated to his official mission. I want a complete list of these people. You can get most of this from the U.S.S.R. Section of the F.B.I. foreign division. They have a special surveillance service for Russian diplomats. They've undoubtedly been following Kirilenko since he left New York. And again, I'd like to know if, in the last few months, Kirilenko has been in touch either by letter or phone with suspicious political or criminal elements. Ask the police to find out from their sources if Kirilenko has had any meetings with members of the 'organisation'. I want an answer before the end of the day."

"Is that all, sir?" The voice of the police officer had a metallic ring.

"No, one more thing. Ask both the New Jersey and New York police for a complete report on the daily activities of Mrs. Olga Petrovna Kirilenko, of 860 Mimosa Drive, Simpson, New Jersey. Find out if she has a car, and if so, does she often drive it alone. Find out if she left her house the night of the murder, at three a.m., and if she was away from home last night around midnight. I want a detailed account of her activities during the past two months and any suspicious contacts she might have had during this period. Ask the F.B.I. about her too. They must have a file on her. That's all."

Pattison beckoned Shuvakin who was eager to interrupt his botanical observations and return to the car. He asked no questions.

"I called to check on whether the two Kirilenkos had alibis for the nights of the murders."

Shuvakin said nothing. The green light flashed on the car radio. Pattison picked up the receiver.

"B 33 here, I'm listening."

"Headquarters to B 33. I have an urgent message for you, sir. You and Mr. Shuvakin have been asked to go to Washington this afternoon. You are expected at the White House at eight o'clock. I repeat: eight o'clock. The Secretary of State, the chiefs of the special services and Ambassador Gaidukov have also been summoned to the meeting. A car will pick you up at the Soviet delegation at six p.m. and take you to a special plane at La Guardia airport. That's all."

Shuvakin looked at Pattison. "What do you make of that?"

Pattison took a large cigar from his breast pocket, tore off the cellophane wrapper, bit off the end and spat it angrily out of the car window. "What I make of that is that the man in the White House is getting impatient." He turned on the ignition and pumped the accelerator until the engine roared.

"This is in no way an official meeting," the President said. "That is why I decided to hold it in the Blue Room." He smiled, but he was obviously very tense.

Paco Ramirez, the Philippine photographer assigned to the

White House, appeared at the door, supple and silent as a shadow. "Not tonight, Paco," the President said.

Pattison leaned towards James Dolan, the President's adviser on national security affairs. "If you'd told me three days ago that there'd ever be a meeting like this one, I would have eaten my hat." Dolan gave him a tight smile.

Sitting in a row on the large couch facing the President's desk were Dimitri Gaidukov, Sergei Shuvakin and Alexei Lavrentiev. Lavrentiev was the Soviet Ambassador to Washington. A career diplomat, he was a timid, fussy man with no initiative, which was why Washington preferred to deal directly with Gaidukov. Although he was officially in New York, Gaidukov had early on become the actual Soviet representative in the United States.

Stanley Hobbs, the Secretary of State, was sitting on the President's right. In a semi-circle near them sat James Brodke, the New York Chief of Police, Art Bailey, head of the F.B.I, and Harold (Hal) Richards, head of the C.I.A. Not in their wildest dreams had the Soviet diplomats ever imagined that they would take part in a secret meeting with the head of the C.I.A. Richards' presence was proof positive that the President was putting all his cards on the table.

The President started right in: "This afternoon, Ambassador Lavrentiev brought me an urgent message from the President of the Soviet Council of Ministers, Mr. Vassili Kuznietzov. The message is very stern indeed. President Kuznietzov does not mince words over his displeasure with our efforts in the Ponomarev affair. He was informed this morning of the murder of the chauffeur..." the President quickly glanced at the papers in front of him "...Arkadi Slobodin. President Kuznietzov expresses his shock at what he calls the 'negligence' of American internal security and wonders how the American government would have reacted if its top representatives and their assistants had been murdered in the middle of Moscow. The President goes on to say that the second assassination reinforces the belief in Moscow that this is an anti-Soviet plot promoted by people in top American circles. He adds that the mounting pressure on him to recall all Soviet diplomats from the United States seriously compromises the Zurich Conference. He concludes with the statement that if the mystery of the two murders is not solved in the next few days, the U.S.S.R. will have to assume the worst, and that relations between the two countries will be in serious jeopardy."

Dolan leaned towards Pattison: "Kuznietzov is in a real bind. He went out on a limb for this Zurich Conference, but the Army is putting the pressure on him and this business makes him their prisoner."

There was a buzz of Russian from the couch. The President put the papers down on his desk, took off his glasses and looked around at each man. "Gentleman, I asked you here primarily to hear that message. But I have something else I want to say." The President leaned forward in his chair, and the note of official concern turned to one of personal urgency. "I am referring to the Zurich Conference, to my hopes and my country's. It was a principal theme of my campaign; it is the program by which my administration stands or falls. I want the Zurich Conference to take place. I want an end to the arms race that has cursed our two countries for a generation. Our two peoples—Russian and American—are sick to death of it. We have better things to do with our brains, our energies, our money. And I have had President Kuznietzov's wholehearted support in this." Now his voice was really vibrating: "I want you to understand that I will not allow the events of the last two days to threaten this program."

He stopped, and his body relaxed. The next words were addressed to Gaidukov: "As you know, the moment the Minister's body was found, we set up a special investigating team composed of the most experienced men in our internal security service. They have had complete co-operation from the Soviet delegation to the U.N. I have invited the head of the team to come here tonight and give us a report on the current status of the investigation. It is the only way I know to convince you of the good will and good faith of the American government."

Lavrentiev suddenly came alive. "Why should we be interested in an interim report? Mr. President, it is absolutely out of the question for us to consent to such a procedure. This might be a deliberate maneuver on your part to make the representatives of the U.S.S.R. in Washington subscribe to conclusions which in fact camouflage the manifest guilt of the United States. I cannot lend myself to such a maneuver." The President stiffened. "Mr. Ambassador, I have done my best to prevent this crisis from breeding any bitterness. I will not tolerate anyone in this room making malicious insinuations about the integrity of the United States. Nor have I the least intention of asking you to subscribe to the commission's conclusions. If this is what you're afraid of, and if you consider this meeting an American attempt to draw you into a trap, you are entirely free to get up and leave the room. All I had in mind was that we listen together to a first-hand report of what has been accomplished so far, and to try to find means, if there are any, to speed up the investigation. As I told you at the beginning, this is not an official meeting. Nobody is committed to anything. I have no intention of asking for your approval or your signature on the report."

Gaidukov leaned towards his colleague and said in a calm voice: "I think it would be a good idea to hear what my friend, Mr. Pattison, has to say to us."

There was a palpable sense of relief in the room. With a few well-chosen words, Gaidukov had saved the meeting from going up in smoke. Lavrentiev was pale with rage, but he did not dare reply to his colleague's affront.

Bill Pattison opened his briefcase and pulled out a sheaf of papers. Briefly and concisely, he described every detail of the investigation. He dwelt particularly on the Minister's relations with Olga Kirilenko, on his interrogation of her and the results of his enquiries into the two Kirilenkos' activities during the past few days.

"These reports came in just before I left for Washington. Our conclusions are categorical: Mr. and Mrs. Kirilenko have no connection whatsoever with either murder. We are convinced that Mr. Kirilenko never left the midwest." The three Russians on the couch looked visibly relieved. "And Mrs. Kirilenko's alibi is watertight. She does drive and she uses her husband's car when he is away. But the car has been laid up in a garage since the beginning of the week. We checked out the local taxis and buses, we interrogated neighbours and the local police. There is no evidence that Mrs. Kirilenko ever left her house at the time of either murder. There remains the possibility that for one reason or another —Mr. Kirilenko's jealousy, Mrs. Kirilenko's frustration with her love affair—one of them might have hired a third party to commit the murders. It is very difficult to prove anything definitive in this area, but from everything we know, it seems highly unlikely.

"You asked me, Mr. President, if we had come to any preliminary conclusions. I have to admit that the double murder is still a mystery to us. But I have a few hypotheses based on what we know. If you will permit me, I should like to outline them for you.

"The first possibility is that the Minister was killed by either Mr. or Mrs. Kirilenko or a killer hired by them; in that case, the chauffeur, Slobodin, would have been killed to prevent him from telling what he knew about the relations between the Minister and Mrs. Kirilenko. As I've already said, we have rejected this hypothesis.

"Second possibility: that the Minister was a victim of armed robbers who had no idea who he was. But then, why should they have killed Slobodin the next day? This hypothesis cancels itself out.

"Third possibility, and altogether plausible: a political murder. Someone with an interest in eliminating the Soviet Foreign Minister. We have many refugees from Eastern European countries here. We also have several groups of anti-Soviet extremists. Perhaps some foreign power hired professional assassins to kill the Minister. Perhaps it was some kind of provocation: kill the Foreign Minister on American soil and so torpedo relations between Washington and Moscow. I'm not giving away secrets when I say that there is at least one power which might be very interested in doing just that."

Dolan and Gaidukov exchanged knowing smiles.

"But there's still something wrong," Pattison went on. "Had that been the case, we would be dealing with a carefully planned murder—everything worked out to the nth degree. Instead we have exactly the opposite. The murder couldn't have been prepared long in advance because hardly anyone knew the Minister was coming to New York. His visit was announced in the press only the day before his arrival. Which means that the murderers had practically no time to prepare the crime. Then there is another problem: how could the killers know that the Minister was going alone in the middle of the night to a secret rendezvous with Olga Kirilenko? After all everyone thought that the Minister was coming to the reception for the Egyptian President. He changed his plans only at the last moment, after talking to Mrs. Kirilenko. The Plaza switchboard tells us that he put in his call to New Jersey at six o'clock.

"I find it hard to believe that any organisation could have put its plan into operation in so short a time. It seems to me equally unlikely that professional killers would take the risk of hanging around the Plaza, armed, in a parked car, hoping against hope that the Minister would leave the hotel without his bodyguard. It would be an extraordinary piece of luck for the killers to be in the right place, see the Minister leave the hotel, follow him, set up an ambush and kill him. And even if all that were possible, how do we explain Slobodin's murder? To be sure, Slobodin could have betrayed him, he could have told the assassins that the Minister was on his way to a rendezvous. And the killers would have had to eliminate him to keep him from talking. This explanation seems logical at first glance, but there are too many loopholes. Slobodin was devoted to Ponomarev. My own enquiries and those of Mr. Shuvakin leave absolutely no doubt that Slobodin himself was above suspicion and that he had no contacts with any one remotely suspicious. So there again, we are at an impasse, even though we can't completely dismiss this hypothesis.

"So, what have we left? One last explanation. It may strike you as fantastic, even crazy. But the more I think about it, the more it makes sense. I think Ponomarev was killed by mistake."

In the general consternation that followed, only Hal Richards, head of the C.I.A. reacted calmly. The others registered variously disbelief, scepticism, suspicion or anger. The President seemed the most disturbed of all.

"What are you trying to tell us, Mr. Pattison?" His voice betrayed his irritation.

Lavrentiev was about to say something, then decided against it. Gaidukov leaned forward. Pattison looked straight at the President.

"Mr. President, allow me to explain. All the hypotheses I suggested are full of holes. Only one of them provides a logical explanation for what happened. I believe that the assassins had no intention of killing Minister Ponomarev. It was Slobodin they were after."

"That's impossible!" Shuvakin burst out. "Who on earth would want to kill Slobodin?"

"Just a moment." Pattison was groping for control. "Try to imagine that somebody—for whatever reason—wanted to eliminate Slobodin. I don't know what the reason is yet, but we'll try to find it. Suppose these people had followed Slobodin for several days, that they knew his habits, his routine. They knew his address, but they preferred killing him in an isolated spot.

"The day of the murder, somebody shadows Slobodin. They see him park by the service entrance, get out of the car and enter the hotel. Remember he was wearing a dark suit and did not have on his chauffeur's cap. That was found in the car after the accident. A few minutes later, a man in a dark suit walks out of the Plaza, gets into the car and drives off. From a distance, it would be next to impossible to distinguish between Slobodin and Ponomarev. All the more so because the killers assume that the man who got into the car could only be Slobodin.

"The Lincoln is followed to Olga Kirilenko's house. The killers watch the house until about three when they see a man walk out and get into the Lincoln. They overtake it and set up the ambush. They kill the driver of the Lincoln and return to the city, convinced they've gotten the man they wanted—Slobodin.

"Then next day, they learn their mistake. Their victim was Ponomarev. Catastrophe. They got the wrong man. The police will certainly make extraordinary efforts to catch the assassins. Surveillance of the Soviet delegation headquarters and its personnel will be tightened. The situation is very

34

dangerous. They must clear out fast, but they have to get rid of Slobodin first. He may say too much and if the police learn that he was the target, they may pick up the traces. Curtains. All those carefully laid plans gone down the drain. They follow Slobodin intending to kill him the first chance they get. Hence the midnight ambush in front of his house. The risks are great but they bring it off and get away. They have finally achieved their goal although they killed the Russian Foreign Minister into the bargain."

"It sounds pretty fantastic to me," the President said, shaking his head.

Hal Richards let out a discreet cough. "Mr. President, if I may say something ... I admit that it sounds fantastic, as you say. But on reflection, I also have to admit that it's not implausible. Maybe the thing did happen that way. Maybe it really was a stroke of bad luck. I have a proposition to make: Bill Pattison has done a marvellous job in New York. I suggest he and the F.B.I. continue, with the collaboration of the Soviet delegation, to work on the political assassination theory. I will take on the mistaken murder idea and will use the best men I have to help me check his hypothesis. Of course, on condition that you agree to the idea of two parallel investigations and that Art Bailey has no objection to having my men operate in his private domain."

"What do you think, gentlemen?" The President still seemed doubtful.

"I have nothing against it," the F.B.I. chief said.

The Russians made no comment.

"I would have liked to conduct that investigation myself," Pattison cut in.

"No, Bill," Hal Richards said. "You're doing too well in New York. I think you should stay there."

"O.K. I accept your proposition," the President said. "I'm willing to see you try to prove this theory, even though I think it's crazy. We have nothing to lose by conducting two parallel investigations." Then he turned to the Russians: "I ask just one thing of you: that you report this meeting to your government, and ask President Kuznietzov if he will wait just a few more days—let's say, a week—before he takes steps both of us will regret. I have every hope that a week from

35

now we'll know where we are. But we must avoid any precipitate action. I want to believe that we will still be meeting each other in Zurich. What do you think, Mr. Foreign Minister?"

Smiling broadly, he addressed these last words to Gaidukov. The Russian looked embarrassed. He was about to say something, thought better of it, and smiled back.

With an air of false innocence, the President addressed the company: "I forgot to tell you that just before this meeting, Mr. Gaidukov was asked to return to Moscow. He has been named acting Foreign Minister until the Supreme Soviet names a successor to Mr. Ponomarev. I regret the circumstances that brought it about, Mr. Gaidukov, but please accept my heartiest congratulations and my best wishes for your success."

The President rose, walked over to Gaidukov and shook his hand warmly.

The meeting was over. As each man left the room, he said goodbye to the President and congratulated Gaidukov. Once outside, Art Bailey pulled Hal Richards aside: "The old fox. Did you see how he put them all in his pocket? He's already cast a spell over Gaidukov. I think you can bet your bottom dollar the Russians don't budge for a week."

"I'm sure of it," the C.I.A. chief answered.

"And how do you plan to solve the mystery of the mistaken murder?" Bailey made no attempt to hide his scepticism.

"I have no idea for the moment, but I think I have just the man for the job."

It was two forty a.m. when the telephone rang in Jeff Saunders' apartment.

He had been waiting for the call for months. And he knew it would come just like this: in the middle of the night, without warning, and that a cold, calm voice would say: "Mr. Saunders, Mr. Richards would like to speak with you." Then he'd hear Hal's slightly hoarse voice say: "Hello, Jeff, how are you, old man? It's been a long time. Listen, Jeff. How about getting dressed and coming over to my place for a talk? What do you say?" And Jeff would answer: "So sorry,

36

but I'm terribly busy just now. That's right, isn't it, Sandy? (Or Tina, Shirley, Ann or maybe Virginia)." And she'd murmur: "Yes, Jeff, terribly busy." And he'd say: "You see, Hal, she's against it. Maybe some other time." And he'd drop the receiver in its cradle.

His little revenge. He knew it was stupid and childish, but that's the way he imagined it. They'd come begging, and he'd be unavailable. After what they'd done to him, after that brutal kick in the ass, they thought they only had to whistle and he'd come running.

But that night, there was no Tina, no Shirley, not even Virginia. There was only a half-empty bottle of whisky on his bedside table, with another one—empty—somewhere under the bed. Paperbacks lay scattered around, a three-day accumulation of half-eaten T.V. dinners was piled on the table along with dirty glasses and cigarette butts. As he picked up the phone, he realised he hadn't shaved for two days.

The only other error in his scenario was that the voice at the other end was not some assistant. It was the C.I.A. chief himself.

"Hello, Jeff."

No answer.

"I need you right away, Jeff. Can you get over here in half an hour?"

Saunders had forgotten everything he planned to say— the biting irony, the massive indifference.

"The office?"

"Yes."

"I'll be there."

He ran into the bathroom and stood under the shower, letting the needles of icy water pepper his skin. He sang snatches of commercial jingles as he shaved, then ran back into his bedroom to find clean underwear. Suddenly, he stood still in his tracks and said out loud: "Jeffrey Saunders, aren't you ashamed of yourself? All they have to do is whistle and you come running." But he couldn't suppress the great wave of joy that washed over him. He was prepared to do anything they said to get back in action. His exile was over.

He kicked an empty bottle lying by the door but as he started to leave the room, he took one last nip from the bottle on the bedside table. One for the road.

Hal Richards was waiting for him in his office, flanked by Bill Pattison and Jim Sullivan, chief of operations for the C.I.A. They wasted no time in small talk.

"I can imagine how you feel, Jeff, and I have no intention of making excuses. I'm sure you'd like to have my scalp. Maybe you're right, maybe you're wrong. Maybe you haven't changed your mind about what happened. Maybe I haven't changed mine. But what I want to talk to you about now has nothing to do with all that. I have a proposition to make to you. I need the best brains we have in the service. This job is important. If you don't believe me, I can ask the President of the United States to call you within the next five minutes. But I don't think that's what you want. I think you want a job. And I've got one for you. What do you say?"

"You want me to find out who killed Ponomarev," Jeff said with a small smile.

"As sharp as ever, aren't you, Jeff? You haven't changed. Yes, you're right. I want you to find out who killed Ponomarev. You have a week to do it in. The American government will give you all the help you need. Our own men, the police, the F.B.I., everybody will be at your beck and call. I don't want to overdo the dramatic bit, but maybe the future of the United States depends in large measure on your success."

Jeff decided it was no time for jokes.

"O.K., I'll do it." Then he decided to go the whole way. There was a moment of silence while he looked Richards in the eye. "I'll do it on one condition: that it will be my mission, from start to finish. No assistants, no bosses. I will want your men, the police, the F.B.I., only when I ask for them. Is that clear?"

This was too much for Richards. "Goddammit, Jeff! This operation is of crucial importance. You can't demand..."

Relaxed, Saunders let a panatella. "I do demand, Hal. Take it or leave it."

The head of the C.I.A. looked at him fixedly. He seemed to be weighing something. Then he abruptly changed gears and reverted to the cool man of action. "O.K. I accept. Now let's go into Jim's office. You know Bill Pattison, don't you?"

Jeff nodded. "We're old friends."

"This is the plan: Bill has a very interesting theory about Ponomarev's murder. He thinks it was a mistake. He'll tell you all about that. He has a complete file and he'll bring you up to date on all the details, everything he's done up to now—investigations, interrogations and all that. You and Jim will decide on how you want to work out your co-ordination with the F.B.I. and the others. I promised the F.B.I. you'd keep out of each other's hair." He smiled and put out his hand: "Good luck, Jeff. If you run into any problems, anything urgent, don't hesitate to call me here or at home. Any time."

It was daybreak by the time Jeff left Jim Sullivan's office. His head felt heavy with all the information he had just assimilated. Bill Pattison liked to get to the bottom of things. He had covered every tiny detail during their long conversation. Then, to make sure Jeff forgot nothing, he gave him the reports and tapes of every conversation and interrogation having anything to do with the murder. "Strange idea," Jeff said to himself. "Murder by mistake. But you never know. Bill isn't one to go off half-cocked. He sounded pretty convincing."

Saunders needed sleep now, but he wasn't going to get it. As he slid between the sheets of his unmade bed, the phone rang. He recognised Jim Sullivan's voice. The C.I.A. operations chief was very excited. "Jeff, there's a new development."

"What's happened?"

"We told you about ordering an investigation of all the police records to see if we could track down more bullets from a .32 calibre Winchester Special?"

"Yes. Bill told me about it. Well . . . '"

"The Florida police have just informed me that a man was killed ten days ago in his cabin at the Cabana Club of the Hotel Dauphine in Miami Beach. They haven't got the murderer yet, but they found two bullets from a .32 Winchester Special in the dead man's body."

"The same rifle?"

"The very same. The ballistics examination proves it."

"Who was the victim?"

"A wealthy middle-aged bachelor named Steven Dragner."

Jeff was silent for a moment. "That's fantastic. Maybe Bill Pattison is on the right track after all."

"This means you leave for Miami in forty minutes. A car is on its way to your apartment. You have a seat reserved on Eastern's Flight 603. Get going."

"God, I haven't any clean clothes."

"Take dirty ones and have them cleaned in Miami. If your plane isn't hijacked to Cuba, you should be there at nine forty-five. Good trip and don't pinch the stewardesses' asses."

"Go to hell," Jeff bellowed into the phone, but Sullivan had already hung up.

3

THE VIEW FROM THE NINTH FLOOR OF THE DAUPHINE AT
Miami Beach was very impressive. The white horseshoe-
shaped building gleamed in the morning sun. Between its
two wings was everything a man could dream of for the ideal
vacation spot. The hotel was surrounded by vast lawns and
flowerbeds worked in intricate geometrical patterns. Winding between these patches of brilliant colour were paths of
carefully raked fine white sand. In the centre was an olympic-
size swimming pool, full of swimmers, and around the edge
guests lay sipping iced drinks served by boys in white uniforms. To the left, the ocean waves lapped lazily against the
immaculate beach dotted with multi-coloured umbrellas.
Opposite, on the other side of the pool, was the long two-
story building called the Cabana Club. Its spacious cabins
opened on the pool, and Jeff could just make out figures
lying on white chaises, others playing cards, still others being
worked over by Cuban masseurs, white towels over their
shoulders.

"What a great place to die!" Jeff said.

"Wonderful advertisement," said the Miami police chief
with mild sarcasm.

"God forbid!" said the hotel manager, David Wolinsky,
and everybody laughed.

The balcony of room 908 was crowded. Everybody who
had met Saunders' plane was there: the Miami police chief,
the head of the criminal division, the chief detective and two
of his men, two police officers, an F.B.I. man and his assistant.

41

Not to mention the obviously worried manager of the Dauphine, the chief clerk and one of the hotel detectives.

"You say the shots came from this room?" Jeff asked the police chief.

The chief of the criminal division answered for him: "We're absolutely certain. Take a look. Dragner was shot while he was lying on the chaise in his cabin at the Cabana Club, Cabin 217, the fourth from the left, the only empty one over there. We had it sealed off but we opened it up this morning for you. We've calculated the angle: the shots had to come from here."

"But if at the moment of the shooting, Dragner was in a slightly different position, the angle of fire would have indicated another room, right?"

"We thought of that, Mr. Saunders. All the other rooms were occupied and their occupants have perfect alibis. This was the only empty room."

"Funny coincidence, don't you think?"

"Not really. We can explain that too. In any case, we found traces of powder on the draperies."

"Where was the murderer standing?"

"I'll show you." He slid the two large glass doors together until they almost met, then closed the draperies until there was an opening barely two inches wide. The room was suddenly thrown in darkness. The air-conditioning made it pleasantly cool after the heat of the balcony.

"The murderer stood about here, say, a foot from the door with the barrel of the rifle in the gap between the curtains. You would never notice it from outside." The officer turned to one of his men. "Jack, hand me the rifle. Thanks. This here is a Winchester Special, exactly the same model as the one used in the murder. Hand me the lens, please." He mounted the telescopic lens on the rifle and held the butt against his shoulder. "Try it yourself, Mr. Saunders. If you aim from here, you can't miss."

Saunders took the rifle, put his eye to the lens, and aimed it until the fine white cross in the centre coincided with the chaise in Cabin 217. "Yes, it really does look like child's play."

"He may even have used a tripod," the officer continued. "This rifle comes with one that's light and collapsible and can be extended to five or six feet. At the time of the murder, Dragner was asleep on his chaise. The doors to his cabin were open. Nothing simpler than to set up a tripod, rest the rifle on it, adjust it and pull the trigger."

"What about the noise? Didn't anybody hear anything? What about the people around the pool?"

"The pool is closed at that hour. It closes every night at six. But the Cabana Club people can stay longer. It's the best time of day to take a rest. Nobody in the pool, everything nice and quiet. Also, the help at the Club is mostly gone by then. The hotel windows overlooking the pool are usually closed; people are down having dinner or watching T.V. Dragner was shot at seven forty-five. The man in charge of the cabins passed his room twice and didn't notice anything. It wasn't until eight o'clock when just about everybody had gone that he looked into 217 and saw that Dragner hadn't budged. Since he always left his cabin before eight, our man went in to wake him and found he was dead."

"But I asked you if anybody heard the shooting. After all, a rifle makes a lot of noise."

"Not all that much, really. Besides, the killers hit on a clever solution. 'The Wild, Wild West' is on television at that time, and it's full of Indians screaming and guns firing. The people in the neighbouring rooms told us the television was on full blast, but otherwise they didn't hear anything unusual. Also, the killers used every pillow and blanket in the room to insulate the door leading into the hall, and all the faucets in the bathroom were on full."

"Which would indicate they had planned things very carefully."

"That's right, Mr. Saunders. Mr. Mitchell of the front desk will tell you how the murderers made sure they had a room overlooking Steven Dragner's cabin."

Mr. Mitchell was eager to oblige: "Now, we get a number of reservations by phone. We have guests who want the same room each year. They either write or telephone to reserve the room. Since the season doesn't begin until October 15th, we can generally satisfy most customers at this time of year. Two weeks before the murder, on August 1st to be exact, we received a telephone call reserving room Number 808 for a week starting August 13th. The client told us he would be arriving late at night and sent us a deposit to cover a night's stay."

"In what form did he send the money?"

"Three ten-dollar bills with a brief typewritten letter. It was postmarked Chicago."

"Sending cash by mail is supposed to be against the law," one of the police officers put in, "but it's done anyway. Miami hotels often get cash by mail."

Mr. Mitchell continued: "On August 4th, we received another call; this one was from a woman, asking for room 908 for four days starting August 14th. She also sent cash, this time with a handwritten note, postmarked Montreal. Then, on August 8th, our New York office informed us they had a reservation for room 608 for two weeks, starting August 16th. They had not received a deposit and asked that we keep the room until ten that night. Nobody turned up for any of those rooms."

"Didn't these reservations strike you as odd?" Saunders asked.

"Don't forget this is a very large hotel. We have two thousand rooms. Each day, we get dozens, sometimes hundreds of reservations. It's not unusual for somebody to pay for a room in advance and then not show up."

"Actually we didn't notice any of this until after the murder." This was from the hotel detective. "It wasn't until we started looking into what rooms had a good bead on Cabin 217 that we realised the killers had three different rooms one above the other covering the 13th through the 16th of August. The maids make up the rooms before one o'clock, so any time after that, you're sure not to be disturbed. And the doors can be opened with any pass-key."

"I assume that the letters told you nothing?" Saunders asked the chief of police.

"Nothing but postmarks and phony names."

The head of the criminal division broke in: "We think we've reconstructed the crime, if you would like to hear it."

"Please do," Saunders said.

"Everything indicates that the murder involved two people —a man and a woman—the ones who reserved the rooms.

44

One or both must have come down and stayed at the Dauphine during the second half of July. They started observing Steven Dragner and noticed that he came to the Cabana Club every day like clockwork. They must have figured out which rooms had the best vantage point for the murder. Then they went back up north and made their reservations. We were able to trace the telephone calls: the first one was made from a public booth in Chicago. The second, the woman's, from a public booth in Montreal. The third one, the call to our New York office, was made in New York, but we haven't been able to trace it.

"Now, notice that Montreal, Chicago and New York are all easily reached by plane. It's very possible that the murderers got on the plane in Montreal—or even in Europe—and stopped off at the airports just long enough to make their telephone calls and mail their letters. Obviously, they used assumed names.

"In any case, it would seem that on the first date, the thirteenth of August, something didn't work out. Maybe Dragner didn't go to the Club that day, or they weren't ready, or something. On the fourteenth, they got into this room, shot Dragner, scored a bull's eye and beat it."

"How did they manage to leave the hotel?"

The chief of police shrugged. "There are a thousand ways. One or both of the murderers might have been staying at the hotel under other assumed names. Anyway, you can dismantle a Winchester in less than a minute, put it in a small suitcase or a beach bag, carry it out of the hotel and check it at the airport. Or they could have hidden it in their car, or even sent it parcel post to New York or wherever. It's equally possible that they stayed at another hotel and, with their beach bag, entered the room. The hotel personnel don't know most of the guests and besides, hundreds of people come and go every day."

"I guess that's it, then," Jeff Saunders said. "There isn't anything more we can do here. Thank you, Mr. Wolinsky." The hotel manager bowed, and with an obvious sense of relief, left the room.

"Chief," Saunders said as they headed for the elevators, "could we stop off at your office? I'd like to ask your men a few questions about the victim. Who this Steven Dragner was, what he did and all that."

"He called himself Steven Dragner from the time he arrived in the United States. His real name was Stepan Dragunsky. He immigrated about fifteen years ago."

"Dragunsky?" Saunders stopped in his tracks. "Where did he come from originally?"

"He came here from Italy, but originally he was from Odessa in the Soviet Union. Steven Dragner was Russian. Didn't we tell you that, Mr. Saunders?"

It was two thirty when Jeff Saunders left police headquarters. The heat of the sun was at its fiercest as Saunders made for a small restaurant across the street. He sat down at a table, ordered a sandwich and a glass of beer and closed his eyes.

Where was he now? Three hours ago, walking into Miami police headquarters, he had been full of hope. He had thought he was on the right track, heading straight for a solution to the mystery. Dragunsky, Slobodin and Ponomarev were all Russians. "It can't be just a coincidence," he'd said to himself. "The key to the mystery must be there." But after three hours of probing interrogation, he had come up with nothing. Zero. From what they told him, Dragunsky had slipped into the West at the end of World War II. He was then thirty-eight, a vigorous man. He spent two years in camps for displaced persons in Italy, living off smuggling and the black market. By 1950 he had saved enough to buy a small boat. For the next five years, he operated along the French and Italian coasts. He was suspected of smuggling, but no one ever caught him at it. In 1955, thanks to the help of relatives who had come to New York right after the Russian Revolution, he was able to emigrate to the United States and set up shop in Miami. He got a job with an Italian who built pleasure craft. They started with a small yard which soon became a big enterprise. The Italian had a way with money and a lively imagination; the Russian knew the sea. They made a name for themselves in Florida and even beyond—building sail boats, speed boats, yachts. They used their heads, opted for quality over quantity. Their clientele was rich—new rich, old rich—ready to spend that little extra for the best. His partner died in 1969 and Dragner decided to retire. He had a healthy bank account and sound investments. A confirmed bachelor, he had no heirs. Right up to that tragic afternoon of August 14th, he had been an exemplary citizen: Steven Dragner had never committed so much as a minor infringement against United States law, unless you counted a couple of speeding tickets, and he belonged to no political organisation or party. In Miami, he was admired and respected by all.

Saunders had counted on the F.B.I. reports, but they too had come up with nothing. Dragner had no connection of any kind with Soviet nationals or Americans known to be Soviet agents. The F.B.I. representative had told Saunders: "Since he came over to the West, meaning since 1945, Dragner broke off all contact with his former homeland."

Jeff left a fifty-cent tip for the Cuban waitress and went over to the public phone in a far corner of the restaurant. He dialled the airport and made a reservation on Eastern's Flight 512 to Washington.

The impersonal female voice at the other end said: 'Please check in at five p.m., sir." He looked at his watch. Two and a half hours until plane time. Just enough for a quick visit to Dragner's place.

It was an attractive one-story house surrounded by a well-kept garden full of tropical plants. Two policemen stood at the front door and a police car was parked near-by. The house was locked, but the police chief had told him he would send over a couple of men in case he wanted to get in.

Saunders was walking along on the shady side of the street and about to cross over to Dragner's house when he was suddenly accosted by a little old lady in a white dress. She gave the two policemen a baleful look and said: "Always sticking their noses in that poor man's affairs. It's not enough that he's been murdered and buried; they still won't let him lie in peace."

Saunders couldn't make out if she was talking to herself or to him. She looked friendly and there was an expression of concern in her sharp brown eyes.

"Did you know Mr. Dragner?" Saunders said with a smile

of encouragement. He knew how nervous and suspicious old ladies could be and was afraid that if she didn't take to him, she might scamper off. But not this lady.

"Did I know Steve Dragner! You bet your life I knew Steve!" And she planted her hands on her hips as if she expected a burst of laughter from an invisible audience. "You can't be from around here if you have to ask that question!" She was silent for a moment then gave him an almost conspiratorial smile: "Steve was one of my very best friends. Yes sir, one of my best. And I tell you what happened to him was horrible, horrible. And you know what I think"— here she leaned closer to him—"I think he was killed by mistake. Yes sir, I think it was a mistake!"

Not that again, not another mistaken murder, Saunders groaned to himself.

The old lady went on: "I bet they wanted somebody in the Mafia. Some smuggler, or I don't know, maybe somebody in the Syndicate. One of those people who come down here to warm their bones in the sun with a million dollars in the bank and a dozen murders on their conscience. The police can't do a thing about those men. But the least they could do is try to protect innocent people like Steve. You must be a stranger here or you'd know the number of criminals we have. I tell you! ... and they aren't petty criminals either!"

Suddenly she stopped. "But who are you anyway? Why should I be telling you all this?"

He bowed and said very politely: "My name is Jeff Saunders, and I work for the government of the United States. In fact, I am one of those trying to solve the mystery of this shocking murder."

"That's the word for it! Shocking!" She looked at him with new interest as she tucked some stray hairs into the bun at the nape of her neck. "So you're a detective? But I thought the investigation was finished?"

"No, we haven't learned anything yet. I was sent especially to find out a few details about Mr. Dragner. So far I've heard only good things about him. What I can't figure out is why anyone would want to do him any harm."

Out of the corner of his eye, he could see that the old lady had taken the bait. There was a moment's hesitation,

48

then she smiled: "I'm Doris Kaplan. Look, it's so hot out here, why don't you come into my house and I'll give you a nice cold glass of beer. My house is right there, next door to Steve's."

There was none of the smell of airless poverty or life on the wane that characterised the houses of so many old people who had come to end their days in the Florida sunshine. Mrs. Kaplan's house was full of light and air. The furniture was modern, the walls hung with brightly coloured pictures. Saunders sat down in one of her comfortable chairs and cheerfully accepted the foaming glass she set in front of him.

"Have some peanuts. Or would you like me to make you a sandwich? You look tired." Mrs. Kaplan scurried about, brought him crackers, pretzels, another glass of beer. "When I saw you, I said to myself right away: 'Here's another nice Jewish boy looking for a house for his parents.' That's what I thought." She gave a little laugh. "But you know, it's one of our faults: we Jews have a tendency to see Jews every where, especially when it's a polite and well-brought up boy like you."

He laughed with her, and gently shifted the subject. "You say you knew Steve Dragner well?"

"I certainly did. A marvellous man. Absolutely marvellous. You know, he came here at least twice a week—sometimes more—to have a drink, chat a bit, watch television with me. Sometimes we played gin rummy together; sometimes he even brought over a friend or two. And sometimes he invited me over to his house. He was so friendly. You know, they say the Russians have split personalities: one side hard and cruel—really horrible; the other, warm and full of love. Well, Steve was all love. He was a good and faithful friend. I'm going to miss him, I can tell you."

Then she added: "You know, I think the real tragedy of his life was that he never married. All his life he was alone. No wife, no parents, no children. Such a marvellous man, but all alone. And don't think he couldn't have married if he wanted to. But there was something that stopped him. He didn't want to start a family."

"Is that your son?" Saunders pointed to a somewhat faded photograph standing on a shelf.

"Oh no. I have three daughters. All pretty, all married, married to good boys, Jewish boys. I have six grandchildren. Every month, one of my daughters comes to visit me with her children. Since the death of my husband—God rest his soul—they see to it that I'm never alone too long."

She grew serious. "No, the boy in the picture is my brother. He died when he was about your age. It was a terrible thing. He went to Poland two months before the Second World War started, to visit our parents. They were Polish, you know, from Warsaw. The war broke out when he was there and he didn't want to leave them." Her eyes began to fill with tears. "Well, you know the rest: the yellow star, the ghetto, then the concentration camp. He died at Auschwitz with the whole family."

"I'm very sorry, Mrs. Kaplan," Saunders said.

"Well, the past is past. Why should I be telling you all this?" She sighed and wiped her eyes. "It all seems so far away, so unreal when you're sitting here in Florida. So few people are capable of imagining that horror. So few. But Steve Dragner could. He was one of those who could. After all, he'd been through it too."

"He'd been through what?" Saunders' mind had been wandering.

"Concentration camp. He'd been there too. For three years."

"At Auschwitz?"

"No, he'd been at Dachau. But it's all the same thing."

Saunders was suddenly alert. "Dragner was at Dachau?"

"Yes. What's so strange about that? Of course it surprised me too the first time he told me. He'd never mentioned it to anybody. Then, all of a sudden, one night ... I was talking about my brother who died over there. He suddenly leaned towards me, put his hand on my arm and said: 'I know only too well what you feel, Doris. I was at Dachau. For three years. It was hell.' I asked him: 'Why didn't you ever tell me?' and he said: 'I never told anybody. It's one of those things you don't like to think about. It was a nightmare.' And then he told me how he'd been a soldier in the Red Army, then in the Navy and had been taken prisoner with his entire crew in the Baltic Sea. He was sent to Dachau. By some miracle he lived through it and when the war was over, he got into Italy. In Italy, things began to look up for him ..."

Saunders had stopped listening. Dachau. Could it be? Was it possible that he held the missing link in his hand? He remembered what Tania Slobodin had told Pattison: "He was moved from one prisoner-of-war camp to another, finally ending up at Dachau ..."

Like a sleepwalker, he got up, muttered a few words of farewell and strode out into the torrid heat of the street.

Dachau!

Six hours later, exhausted, sweating, his clothes sticking to him, Jeff Saunders staggered onto a Pan American 747 at Kennedy Airport in New York. In seven hours he would be in London; two hours later, Vienna, with Egon Schneider.

He sank into his seat and loosened his necktie. Everything was crazy, wild. First, the mad rush back to Miami police headquarters to look over Dragner's file again; then the call to Hal Richards: "Listen Hal, I think I've got something. Two of the three victims were at Dachau at the same time. Maybe Bill Pattison had a point. Somebody may be trying to knock off a group of people who were in that concentration camp thirty years ago. It sounds crazy, but I'm more and more convinced that's what it is."

Richards' excited voice still vibrated in his ears. "Jeff, you've got it! By God, old man, that's got to be it!" Then Richards ticked off the next moves: "You've got to find out what happened at Dachau. Take the next plane. Go to Vienna and see Schneider. He knows you; he'll help you out. I'll send him a cable telling him you're on your way. Then take a plane to Ludwigsburg and the Zentralstelle. They'll help you there too. That's where you'll find the solution, Jeff. I'll send instructions to all our men right away—in Vienna, in Stuttgart—wherever you need help. I'll go tell the President immediately."

Schneider. Vienna. There he was, going back to Vienna, to solve a mystery whose roots reached down into the crematoriums of Dachau, into a nightmare more than a quarter of a century old.

But it wasn't Dachau that sent a shiver down his spine. He

51

was thinking of the first time he'd gone to Vienna, exactly two years ago, and of that terrible night a year later. The memory of that night would be with him for the rest of his life.

4

"WOULD YOU LIKE TO WATCH THE MOVIE, SIR?" A RED-HAIRED
stewardess with a turned-up nose and interminable legs was
leaning over him, giving him the fixed smile she had used at
least a thousand times.

Saunders shook his head. He had neither the strength nor
the desire to waste two hours watching some windless film
put on for the distraction of restless tourists on a voyage of
discovery to the old world. Instead, he asked for a mask and
ear plugs. He put his seat back as far as it would go and
tried to sleep. But the artificial darkness served only to acti-
vate his memories. He remembered how he had felt two
years ago, on his way to Vienna for the first time, like an
exile relegated against his will to some lost corner of the
globe. He was convinced then that he had been the victim
of a terrible injustice. But at the same time, he was aware
that somehow he had stumbled and committed a grievous
error.

It was his first setback. After he had got out of the Marines
and joined the C.I.A., there had been one triumph after another. He attributed his success to his lucky star—the fact
that he was always at the right place at the right time. In
1960, when he was still just a kid, he had helped plan the
U-2 reconnaissance flights over China, the Soviet Union and
the Middle East. It was his idea to send a U-2 over Israel to
photograph· the suspicious building in the Negev Desert
which the Israelis insisted was a textile mill. When the pictures were developed in the C.I.A. labs in Washington, the

experts saw that the "textile mill" was none other than a powerful atomic reactor. And then there was the incident of the "fishing boats" in the North Sea, which turned out to be carrying electronic spying devices under their nets.

Thanks to his mother being French, he was virtually bilingual. Eventually, he was made bureau chief in Paris, and that was when he had met Martine. Warm, seductive, brainy and committed, Martine Duverger had opened his eyes to a new universe. He was excited by his new post; he was excited by this first contact with his mother's native land. And he let Martine seduce him as no woman had ever seduced him before. But he was convinced to this day that for all her cleverness, she never suspected the true nature of his job. That was why he had felt free to follow her wherever she went, meeting all her friends and listening to their talk and their ideas. The next thing he knew, he'd been absorbed into that typically French intellectual atmosphere of scepticism and anti-Americanism. ("You're different," they used to say to him. "After all, you're half French.") It was Martine and her friends from the Sorbonne and Nanterre who first turned him against the Vietnam war, against American capitalism and his country's intransigence towards everything communist. When he was recalled to Washington in 1967, he knew he was already suspected of harbouring dangerous ideas. Some of his colleagues began to avoid him. His brilliant past kept them from firing him outright, but he was no longer allowed access to secret documents relating to the Soviet bloc. "You understand them too well," Jim Sullivan had said to him, halfway between laughter and reprimand. "But I'm not asking you to understand them. I want you to spy on them."

Two days later, Sullivan told him: "The boss thinks it would be a good idea if you worked in another area. He wants you to go to Germany and Austria. We're worried about the success of Adolf Von Thadden's neo-Nazi party. It would be useful if someone with your qualifications looked into its members' past. We don't want to wake up some fine morning with a new Hitler on our hands."

He accepted the mission, but he knew perfectly well he was being shunted to a siding. Why else would they send one of their top experts on Soviet affairs to spy on a bunch of hysterical nuts whose organisation was so weak it couldn't elect a single representative to the Bundestag. But he swallowed his pride and took on the assignment.

That was when he met Schneider. Schneider was a loner, living in Vienna on the edge of poverty, but determined to bring to justice all the Nazis responsible for Auschwitz, Treblinka, Dachau, and all the other concentration camps. Saunders spent whole days with Schneider poring over dossiers meticulously filed in large white boxes. Schneider put him in contact with his friends and the organisations that helped him in his work. Saunders visited all the associations of war victims and former inmates of the concentration camps. He spent long hours in the archives of the Zentralstelle in Ludwigsburg, West Germany's repository for all documents relating to Nazi war crimes. His work had been fruitful: in a few months, he identified over two hundred former Nazi criminals among the members of Von Thadden's party. In the process, he also exposed several old Gestapo and S.S. leaders who had been hiding under assumed names. But he had taken no action against them. From long experience, he knew he wasn't expected to mete out justice or take a moral stand. He was asked only to spy, to furnish information and nothing more.

It was at this time that the Russians began to show an interest in him.

Actually, the Russians' and Saunders' paths had often crossed during his investigations in Austria and Germany. There was nothing surprising about it: the Soviet secret service was also interested in Von Thadden's men—about their past as well as their possible future. He often found himself operating side by side with other "researchers" who unmistakably reported back to Moscow.

It wasn't unusual for special relationships to develop between secret agents working on similar assignments on neutral soil. There was mutual distrust but also a kind of collaboration. During several casual conversations, Saunders hadn't watched his tongue. The "enemy" quickly surmised that they were dealing with a very interesting case: an important American secret agent who was also not unsympathetic to the Soviet Union!

That was how he was eventually chosen for the fateful mission. In early 1969, a young Czech sought Saunders out through the intercession of "a friend of a friend". Observing all the rules of conspiracy, the two met in Salzburg. Saunders was more amused than impressed by the elaborate precautions taken by his opposite number. He hadn't the faintest idea what was wanted of him or the reason for the secrecy about a meeting between two men who had done little more than together leaf through the files of former Nazis. But it was soon evident that the nervous young Czech was after something more than Nazi criminals. Saunders had barely sat down in the car waiting for him in the narrow Salzburg street when the Czech blurted out: "You've got to help me! I'm trying to get Edward Zatek out of Czechoslovakia."

Saunders was silent for several minutes. The proposition had stunned him and he needed time to pull his thoughts together. Edward Zatek was the chief of the Czech secret service. During that heady "Prague spring", Dubcek had kept him at his post and had even included him in the tight little group that ran the country. Zatek was unquestionably a liberal who had accepted Dubcek's ideas on communism and democracy, and supported him wholeheartedly. With the Russians' arrival in Prague in August 1968, Zatek suddenly vanished. Some said he had fled, others that he had been exiled to Siberia. There was even a rumour that the Russians had had him executed. And here was a young Czech on a back street in Salzburg asking a member of the United States intelligence service to help him save Zatek.

Two hours later, he was in his room at the Kaiserhof, tearing up the report he had written on the encounter; he burned it and flushed the ashes down the toilet. He had decided not to tell Washington until he was absolutely certain it wasn't a put-on. If the thing turned out to be a bluff, he would be the only one involved and nobody else would need to know anything. If it were indeed serious, all the more reason to make the preparations on his own and get full credit if it turned out well.

So he got further and further involved in the Zatek lifesaving operation. He had three more meetings with the Czech student who called himself "Walter". Each time he came he was accompanied by his sister Mara, a big plain stoop-shouldered girl. Each time there were new details. When the Soviets first invaded Czechoslovakia, they hadn't touched Zatek. Quite the contrary: they had used him and his apparatus to gain control of the Party and key positions in the various ministries. Zatek had offered no resistance. When Dubcek and General Svoboda returned from their famous trip to Moscow, they asked him to do everything the Russians demanded. They emphasised that Zatek must at all costs hold onto his job. But without any warning, on April 14th, 1969, the Russians removed the chief of secret services and assigned him to the Ministry of Agriculture as head of "long-term planning". Then on July 17th, Zatek was dismissed from this post and exiled to Bratislava where he was given a job as book-keeper in a branch of the "Bata" chain. Zatek, who knew all about gradual liquidation, suspected that his arrest would come in a matter of days. "He is desperate," Walter and Mara had kept repeating. "Each day is another ordeal. We must get him out of Czechoslovakia before it is too late!"

Saunders had demanded definite proof of this account from Walter and Mara—and he got it. They brought him a sheaf of documents including the appointments to his various posts, changes of addresses, police reports on his movements. Then one day, they brought him a handwritten letter from Zatek himself, and Saunders asked if they could arrange a meeting between them. To his great surprise, they could, and did—with extraordinary dispatch. He left for Bratislava using his usual "cover", that of the European representative of an American computer company. He met Zatek in a small shabby apartment in one of the city's poorer districts. "It's a friend's apartment," Zatek told him apologetically. Saunders recognised Zatek immediately, having seen dozens of pictures of him. There was no doubt about it: he was indeed talking to the former head of the Czech secret service. They had a long, frank exchange and as he left, Saunders said: "We will help you."

So the moment had come to tell Washington. He sent a detailed report on his contacts with the two young Czechs and with Zatek, then waited for an answer. In less than twenty-four hours, Elmer Connelly, head of the Czech desk at the C.I.A., was ringing his door bell. "Congratulations, Jeff. You've done a great piece of work. But why didn't you tell us sooner? I'll take personal charge of the operation and I hope you'll help me."

Saunders had wanted nothing more than to help Connelly. In the first place, he would get a piece of the action; in the second, Elmer Connelly was a long-time friend and they had gone through a lot together. So they went to work with enthusiasm. Saunders set up several meetings between Connelly and the young Czechs, and went back to Bratislava for a second interview with Zatek. Finally came the night when Connelly, in the splendid lobby of the Hotel Imperial in Vienna, informed him: "You can tell Walter and Mara that we're ready. Zatek will be picked up on November 17th at four in the afternoon. We'll be waiting at the border. He should make it by November 18th or 19th."

"How are you going to get him out?" Jeff had asked.

Elmer had shrugged. "Sorry, old man, but I can't tell you. You know, secrecy, dark of the night, and so forth ... All I can say is that we've got the best escape network in all Czechoslovakia. Thanks to them, we've been able to get dozens of people out. The Russians are completely fooled." Then he added in a conciliatory tone: "But I promise that you'll be at the head of the receiving line on the Austrian border."

At zero hour, Saunders was in fact flat on his stomach in a pine forest near the Czech border with Connelly and two Austrian agents. At first, he had thought that Zatek would be crossing the border near Bratislava which was close to Austria. But Connelly had another plan: the border crossing would be a hundred or so miles from Bratislava in a craggy section along the Vltava River. The nearest Austrian city was Linz, where they organised the expedition: fur coats, blankets, night binoculars, weapons, hot coffee in Thermos flasks and brandy.

At three a.m., Connelly gave Saunders a friendly tap on the shoulder, laboriously got to his feet and walked through the snow to the other side of the frontier. A vague silhouette detached itself from the dark woods on the Czech side and went to meet him. Then the two men disappeared into the silent forest.

Stretched out in the snow, Saunders had examined the fantastic moonlit landscape—the silent white valley flanked by wooded hills. He wondered about Connelly. Why was he risking himself in Czech territory when he could have waited for Zatek right here? But he knew him well enough to know the answer, to know he had to do it that way, and he—Saunders—would probably have done it too had he been in Connelly's shoes. They liked to execute their missions themselves, less from a sense of responsibility than from the irresistible call of adventure.

"Have you noticed that we haven't seen one of their patrols since eleven o'clock?" It was one of the Austrians talking, and Saunders smiled in the dark. Elmer had mounted a really well-greased operation.

It was at that moment that he noticed a grotesque figure emerging from behind a little hill to the north. It was making strange motions with its arms and leaping awkwardly in the deep snow. Only when the figure had drawn quite near did Saunders understand: it was a man making a desperate attempt to escape, impeded by the snow that reached up to his thighs.

Forgetting all caution, Saunders stood up. "For Christ's sake, why doesn't he go through the forest? Why does he have to expose himself that way? Nobody could miss that target."

As if in answer to his question, a burst of gunfire broke the silence. Saunders saw the blue-red lights exploding from the woods on either side of the valley. Then he knew: the whole thing was a trap. The man was still running down the middle of the valley in the white snow. But he didn't have a chance. A few hundred yards from the border, he collapsed in the snow.

One of the Austrians whispered: "Let's get out of here."

Elmer Connelly didn't come back that night. He stayed stretched out in a pool of blood in the middle of the eerie white valley, an unidentified body, someone who had tried to cross the frontier and hadn't made it. "He was trying to get through to the West," one of the Czech border guards probably said as he examined the corpse.

The next day, there was a paragraph on an inside page of the Austrian papers, noting that "a Czech refugee was killed as he tried to cross the border". At the Hotel Imperial in Vienna, Saunders found Hal Richards waiting for him. Richards was standing rigid, fists clenched, lips tight. He didn't ask Jeff to sit down. After a heavy silence, he said: "I hope you know you're responsible for his death."

Saunders didn't answer.

"Your Russian buddies set you a nice trap. And they killed two birds with one stone. Our Soviet comrades in Prague were beating their brains out trying to figure out a way to close the frontier. How to stop this exodus of Dubcek's men. How were they doing it? What group was helping them? Then somebody said: 'It must be the Americans.' And another said: 'I've got an idea.' And he really did have an idea. He said to himself: 'I know a naïve, mixed-up American who let some French girl fill his head with "progressive" ideas. He's an important C.I.A. agent but he's a little unbalanced. He believes in "good Communists", he's human and he wants to prove himself.' So his little Soviet pals set up a real dilly: they dangled some bait under our young American's nose and the bait was none other than Edward Zatek, Dubcek's chief of secret service who'd sell his mother to the devil to save his own skin. They send two kids fresh out of Moscow's spy school to our nice American; they throw themselves at his feet and bleat 'Save him! Save him!' Our nice American falls for it like a ton of bricks. He does everything they tell him to do, he visits Zatek and swallows all the crap they've dished up for the occasion. He involves his old pal, Elmer Connelly, one of the most brilliant men in American espionage, and Connelly follows his pal with his eyes closed. If his pal says everything is O.K., he must know what he's talking about. After all, he wasn't born yesterday. And then, on November 17th, one of our best Czech agents knocks on Zatek's door. Zatek follows him. From one place to another, from one pair of hands to another, Zatek crosses Czechoslovakia towards the border while the Russian agents follow in his shadow, picking up every man in the

60

Czech network one by one. By the time they get to the border, they think they have them all, but oh no! There's even bigger game waiting for them there—Elmer Connelly. Connelly had trusted his old pal Saunders and thrown himself right into the front line. 'Not bad!' said our Russian comrades. 'We get that one too!' And as Connelly was trying to escape, they mowed him down. Now our nice young American is back in Vienna, and he's looking a little depressed."

Saunders still said nothing. Richards' tone grew even angrier.

"O.K., Saunders: there's a plane to the States at six forty-five tonight. Get on it and don't come back! So far as I'm concerned, you're through!"

From then until the day before yesterday, Saunders had not set eyes on Hal Richards. And the memory of that night when he'd seen his friend struck down at his feet still made him wince with pain.

Saunders was a broken man when he left Vienna that night. For many months, he pondered the episode: he was convinced he had been unjustly punished for what was essentially a human error that anyone might have made. And here he was on his way back to Vienna and his last chance to prove himself—and, O.K., maybe even prevent another world war as well.

He ordered a double Scotch and soon after the Boeing 747 started its slow descent into Heathrow.

5

DURING THEIR PERIOD OF COLLABORATION, SAUNDERS HAD come to know Egon Schneider well and gradually pieced together his story. A small man, Schneider had broad shoulders and a large head, with thick black hair and lively blue eyes. His exuberance made him seem younger than his fifty-two years. He had been through the horrors of Dachau, Auschwitz and Buchenwald, but the Nazi torturers had not been able to break his spirit or blunt his inexhaustible energy.

In 1936, when he was a Viennese schoolboy of eighteen, Egon ran away from home. Six months later, his parents received a first letter. To their astonishment, the envelope had Spanish stamps on it; their carefree schoolboy had joined the International Brigade fighting Franco in Spain. He returned in 1938, scarred, disappointed, but his morale still high. Not long after the Anschluss and Austria's annexation by the Third Reich, he disappeared again to set up an underground organisation of anti-Hitler intellectuals, journalists and writers. In 1940 he was arrested for reasons having nothing to do with his underground activities: in May of the same year—a few weeks before the German war machine rolled into Paris—he had published his first book, a vivid account of the civil war in Spain which caused a small stir in Paris. The critics predicted a brilliant future for the young writer, but not long after the occupation of France, the book fell into the hands of the S.D. (*Sicherheitsdienst,* the secret service of the German Army.) It took the Germans only two weeks to find Schneider and arrest him.

Paradoxically, the Nazis never discovered his underground activities, and this had saved his life. He was deported with a number of other intellectuals to Dachau. In 1943 he was transferred to Buchenwald, and from 1944 until the liberation, he was at Auschwitz.

When he returned to Vienna, he was sought after by every publisher in the city. But he turned down offers that would have made him a rich man. "When I was in Auschwitz," Schneider said at the time, "I swore over the open graves of my dead companions that I would dedicate my life to bringing their murderers to justice. And that is what I intend to do." He sold his family house, and with his young wife, moved into a small house in the Vienna suburbs. He tracked down witnesses, information, documents, and set up an elaborate filing system. First the allied military prosecutors, and later the Austrians and West Germans, learned to appreciate Schneider's thoroughness. He succeeded in identifying hundreds of criminals, from the most notorious executioners to insignificant guards, and saw them brought to justice. More than once, when contributions from former internees had dried up, he was close to hunger, but still he persevered.

When Saunders visited Schneider for the first time in 1968, he had had to wait a long while in the sparsely furnished room on the ground floor. Schneider's young wife had offered him tea, and as he aimlessly patted the family Alsatian, he watched the steady stream of people climbing up and down the creaking stairs to Schneider's study. They were mostly middle-aged, and had come from all four corners of Europe to learn the whereabouts of some relative lost during the war, and always offering some small sum to support Schneider in his work.

Schneider had welcomed him warmly and asked no questions. He offered him access to all his files and refused any sort of payment. When they finally parted, Schneider told him: "If I can ever be of any use to you again, please do not hesitate to ask. I am at your service."

And here he was back in the same room. With only a week to track down the killers, he needed Schneider's help more than ever.

63

"Summer rain," Egon Schneider said with satisfaction. "It is the only rain worthy of the name."

He pulled on his pipe and looked out of the open window. The heavy rain drummed on the branches of the trees outside, and the wet leaves glistened in the reflected light of the study lamp.

"I like heavy drops," he said with a smile. "It reminds me of the tropical rains in books. This is the way it must be there: a sudden hard downpour, then that special smell of washed earth and purified air. Have you ever been in the tropics, Herr Saunders?"

Schneider didn't wait for an answer but instead walked towards the electric kettle whistling in a corner of the room, and carefully heaped two large spoonfuls of Nescafé into two earthenware mugs. Then he poured in the water and added a lump of sugar. "One lump, if I remember correctly," he said, and Saunders nodded.

He placed his mug on a small table in front of the couch, first removing a pile of dark brown folders and setting them on the floor. "Please sit down, Herr Saunders," he said politely.

The room was crammed with dossiers. Hundreds of brown or fading folders, on the desk, on the chairs, on the floor, on shelves, piled between and on top of books. Some were open, revealing papers darkened with age. In one corner stood a pile of wooden crates, one on top of the other. Saunders knew what was in them: the personal records of thousands of Nazi war criminals. Some were now in prison; most had never been found.

Schneider sat down at his desk and shoved a pile of papers to one side. Saunders' telegram lay under the desk lamp. "If this affair you mention in your telegram were not so urgent, I would remind you that you did not take time to send me so much as one postcard in all these many months."

"If this affair were not so urgent, I would make my *mea culpas* and ask a thousand pardons," Saunders said smiling.

Schneider settled back in his chair and let his hands fall on the desk. "Good. Enough protocol. Tell me what brings you here and why it is so very important."

Saunders hesitated for a moment then began slowly: "I

want to check on certain details concerning something that happened at Dachau thirty years ago. I am in the process of investigating a curious incident that involved two Russians who were interned at Dachau during the war. They were soldiers in the Red Army who had been captured by the Wehrmacht."

Was it his imagination, or had he caught a flicker of apprehension in Schneider's eyes when he said the word "Russians"? Was it only his imagination that Schneider stiffened in his chair and held his breath for a second before he folded his hands and asked with measured politeness: "Could you be a little more explicit, Herr Saunders?"

"Unfortunately I cannot tell you more than that. I'm terribly sorry, but please trust me, and do believe me when I say it is of extreme importance. Perhaps of worldwide importance." Saunders gave an embarrassed smile. "However, I can tell you this much: during World War II, something very strange happened at Dachau. Maybe it was something everybody in the camp knew about; maybe it was a minor incident that went by unnoticed; or maybe it was something secret that only a few people were in on. Whatever it was, two Russian prisoners-of-war seemed to be involved. I have their names. I've come to Vienna to ask you to help me find out what happened."

Schneider was silent. Saunders looked at him with concern. There was something mystifying in his old friend's behaviour. His usual good humour had given way to obvious anxiety.

He finally asked: "What are the names of these two men?"

"Stepan Dragunsky and Arkadi Slobodin." Saunders was certain Schneider knew nothing of their murder. There had been nothing in the papers about Slobodin, and Steven Dragner barely made the Miami *Herald*.

Schneider looked at him without expression.

"Is this really such a very serious matter?"

Saunders skirted the question. "Perhaps, at this point, 'serious' is an exaggeration."

Schneider wrote the two names down on a piece of paper. "Unfortunately I can do nothing for you at the moment. As

65

you know, all I have here are the files on the war criminals. What you need are the files on the prisoners so that you'll know what block they were in, and when what you describe happened. Once we know this, we can come back and examine what I have here. The information on Dachau is basically complete. I don't think very much escaped me."

"You have nothing on the prisoners here?"

Schneider smiled. "Dear friend, I myself prepared the files on the Dachau prisoners right after the war. But there are hundreds of thousands of names. You know how many thousands of people went through ... while the 'factory' was working at 'full capacity'. The archives are here in Vienna. I had no room here, so they were stored in steel cabinets in a large room given over to me in the old Rathaus." His tone became bitter: "That was during the period when I was still *persona grata*, when the authorities considered my work a service to the nation—to humanity. Well anyway, the files exist; they're in the basement of the Rathaus. If you like, we can go there tomorrow morning."

Schneider accompanied Saunders to the front door and watched him disappear into the driving rain. Then he returned to his study, took down a slender file from a shelf above his work table and opened it. He read its contents through several times. Then he got to his feet and began to pace back and forth across his study, finally coming to rest before the open window. Motionless, he looked into the night. Then he swung around like a man who has come to a decision, walked over to his desk and picked up the telephone. He dialled long distance, gave the operator a number, and waited.

"I'm ringing your number, sir," the toneless voice said.

But there was no answer at the other end of the line.

The next morning, the two men reached the door to the room in the Rathaus basement, Schneider took some matches from his pocket. He was about to strike one when the custodian who had let them in turned on a switch. An almost blinding white light exposed the room, revealing it to be low ceilinged but spacious, with a faintly mouldy smell.

"See, Herr Schneider," the custodian said, "we had electricity put in. Now that you come here so often, you'll be able to work more comfortably. Those gas lamps gave barely enough light for a museum."

He picked up the two lamps from a metal table in the centre of the room and started for the door.

"Many thanks," Schneider said.

Saunders watched his friend. Once again he was disturbed by Schneider's tension. He seemed tired as well; they had barely spoken since their early morning meeting.

"These are the archives," Schneider said.

Old metal filing cabinets with remnants of green paint lined the walls. Each had a label with a letter of the alphabet.

Schneider did not take off his hat or raincoat which was buttoned up to his chin. He marched straight to a cabinet facing the door and scanned its labels. Then he pulled one of the drawers towards him and started to riffle through with expert hands.

"Here you are. I have one of your Russians." And he read out: "Dragunsky, Stepan. Number KG/435627. Country of origin: U.S.S.R. Military, Sergeant in the Baltic Fleet of the Red Army. Served on board the destroyer *Sverdlovsk*, sunk in June, 1942, by a German submarine in the Gulf of Finland, off the coast of Esthonia. Taken prisoner with other sailors from the destroyer. Deported to Dachau in 1942 where he stayed until the liberation, April 15th, 1945. Until May 1944, interned in Block No. 7; from then until the liberation, in Block 13. After his liberation and convalescence, refused repatriation and found refuge in a camp for displaced persons near Tarvisio, Italy."

"That's all I have on him," Schneider said. "The files are complete only up to July, 1946."

Saunders shook his head in frustration. Schneider walked briskly to another cabinet and pulled out a drawer. "Sab ... Sed ... Slobodin. Here we are: Slobodin, Arkadi: KG/752698. U.S.S.R. Military. Sergeant-Major in the Second Byelorussian Division. Taken prisoner near Kiev in November, 1941. Interned in the prisoner-of-war camps at Katowice, Leipzig..."

Schneider looked up. "It's a long list. Do you want them all?"

"Not for the moment," Saunders said. "Maybe later if I get stuck."

Schneider resumed: "Transferred to Dachau in September 1944. Interned in Block No. 13."

Saunders started. "Block 13! Both were in Block 13!"

Schneider continued: "At the time of the liberation, April 15th, 1945, he asked to be returned to the U.S.S.R. He had a long convalescence then took a Red Cross train to the U.S.S.R. via Poland. That's all there is."

"Both were in Block 13," Saunders repeated. "And at the same time. From September '44 until the liberation. Do you have anything on that period?"

"Yes." Schneider walked over to three smaller files in a far corner of the room. The labels on the drawers had numbers instead of letters.

"Actually, I have a copy of these files—each block has a file to itself—at my house," Schneider said. "But it would be better to look at them here. We might find the names of other prisoners whose records would be here."

As he talked, he pulled out one drawer after another. Finally, in a lower drawer, he found a thick file which he placed on the table. On the cover, printed in red ink, was the inscription: "Block 13, Dachau."

"How good is your German?" Schneider asked as his eyes ran over the yellowing pages.

Saunders sighed. "I speak it fairly fluently but reading, not so good."

"That's what I thought."

Schneider returned to his examination of the file. Saunders sat down on a rickety chair, took a box of panatellas from his pocket and lit one. He knew Schneider liked to work in silence and hated people peering over his shoulder.

The Austrian finished his reading with amazing speed. "Most of these documents are of little interest. Block 13 was a small wooden barracks with wooden cots. There were as many as five hundred prisoners in the other blocks, but in Block 13, there were only about fifty at the beginning. All Germans: Communists, Socialists, Catholics, liberals. All political prisoners. Towards the middle of 1942, they began adding French prisoners—members of the Resistance, mostly.

By May, 1944, there were hardly any Germans left in the block. Most of them had been exterminated, or had simply died. A few were transferred to other camps. That's when they decided to lock up prisoners-of-war in Block 13 as well. So, to the handful of French still there, they added Russians and Polish prisoners. Soon they had two hundred and fifty men. You can imagine the appalling conditions they lived in."

Schneider thought for a moment. "I'm sure they put the Russians and Poles together on purpose. They knew the two couldn't stand each other. Probably they assumed they'd kill each other off. From what I have here, it seems the block was under the supervision of one of the worst assassins at Dachau, Sturmführer S.S. Joakim Müller. A real monster —the prisoners called him 'Satan'. He disappeared after the war; we've lost all trace of him. He probably lives in a neat little house, runs an insurance agency, and heads the local society for the prevention of cruelty to animals in his spare time."

He continued his examination of the file. "Ah, here is something that might interest you. It's the report of a United States Army major, describing Block 13 as he found it at the time of the liberation."

He handed Saunders a photocopy of the typewritten document. The heading read "United States Army". It was signed by Major George O'Hara, a staff officer with the Eighth Division Headquarters. Dated April 30th, 1945, the document was inscribed: "Dachau Extermination Camp; Block 13".

The style was dry, succinct, almost cold. Saunders took an instant dislike to Major O'Hara, imagining him to be a heavy thick-set Irishman without a shred of compassion. Then it occurred to him that what the major had seen must have struck him with such horror that he resorted to dry, impersonal language to escape the nightmare.

I arrived at the Dachau concentration camp near Munich towards noon on April 15th, 1945. The camp was already under American military control. Two regiments of the Eighth Army had occupied it at dawn without firing a shot. There were stories from survivors and from our intelligence that on April 9th the German guards had joined up with a retreating armoured column of the Wehrmacht and left the internees to their own devices.

As soon as I arrived at the camp, I presented myself to the Division Command which had taken up temporary quarters in the Kommandantur Building. There were already several staff officers there. We were summoned into an office where Colonel Masters, a Division staff officer in charge of special missions, brought us up to date. He briefed us on the nature of the camp, described what the S.S. had done there, and called our attention to the physical and moral condition of the survivors. Then each of us was assigned to inspect a block, make a list of the survivors, describe their condition and try to ascertain their needs. We were to finish those reports the same day.

I was assigned to Block 13, and was accompanied by Doctor Brown of the 743rd Regiment who had been transferred to Dachau. On the way we passed piles of corpses, most of them naked. Corpses were scattered along the roads, looking like skeletons with only skin left on them. Doctor Brown said most of them had died of starvation and exhaustion.

Block 13 is in the south-west sector of the camp. It's the last in a row of four blocks numbered 13, 14, 15 and 17. The four blocks are surrounded by a barbed wire fence. A sign at the entrance to this group of blocks says *Kriegsgefangene*, which means "Prisoners of War". However, Captain Penton of the 734th Regiment, who was there when we arrived, said that there were a few French and Dutch political prisoners mixed in with Russian and Polish prisoners-of-war.

Block 13 is a rectangular barracks, smaller than the others in the group. There was a pile of corpses in front of the door. Prisoners from the other blocks who were standing around (we talked to them through an interpreter) appeared unmoved at the sight of the bodies. In answer to our questions, they told us they were used to living among the dead.

As I entered Block 13, I immediately saw that there

were very few survivors. Only two were still able to stand; the rest were lying motionless on the wooden planks they used as beds.

We quickly realised that most of the men lying on the planks were dead. Sergeant Kransky of the 824th Regiment who had been assigned to us as interpreter, talked to one of the prisoners in Polish. He was told that they had all died during the last four days, between the time the Germans fled and the Americans arrived. He told us that the condition of the men in this block was especially bad because they'd had only subsistence rations. Up to April 9th, the death rate in Block 13 had been between five and ten a day. After the departure of the Germans, the inmates in the other blocks started looking around for food, but the men in Block 13 were too weak to walk and therefore couldn't go foraging food. As a result, about seventy died of hunger in the space of four days.

We counted the number of survivors in the block: there were sixty-three, all of them in pitiful condition. About fifteen men, including the two who could still stand, lay on planks behind a wooden partition at the far end of the barracks. They included Russians, Poles, a Frenchman and two Dutchmen.

I asked one of the Polish prisoners why the inmates of Block 13 seemed to be in worse condition than the others. He told me that their treatment had been especially harsh because they were Russian and Polish prisoners-of-war. Although they hadn't suffered the fate of the Jewish prisoners who were asphyxiated in gas chambers and then thrown into ovens, their rations were kept very meagre with the apparent intention of starving them to death. He told how difficult it was, particularly in winter, when the inmates were still capable of violence. The hunger drove many of them mad. Terrible fights broke out over a spoonful of soup or a piece of bread. More than a few were killed during these fights. These finally stopped when the prisoners became too weak to make the physical effort.

I made a list of survivors, according to the numbers on their uniforms, and Doctor Brown—with the help of two

71

orderlies—immediately set to work treating the most severe cases. The company canteen furnished special rations which we distributed in small quantities in line with the doctor's orders. Even so, ten more died that day.

As officer in charge, I had the dead removed and the survivors disinfected by a sanitation team. Clothes and blankets were provided. They all received intensive medical care, vaccinations and vitamins. Their condition was so bad, however, that in spite of our efforts, twenty-five more died before the end of the month. Only twenty-eight inmates of Block 13 are still alive.

The report ended there. Saunders stared at the folder in his hands. Not a clue to the mystery. He looked for Schneider who was in a corner, leaning over one of the open drawers. As Saunders picked up the pages he had been laying on the table, he noticed another page stapled to the report. Its heading read: "List of survivors of Block 13, Dachau, as of June 30th, 1946." There followed a numbered list of names. The last was No. 23, which must have meant that another five died during the year following liberation. He took out his notebook and began to copy down the names. A curious detail caught his attention: small crosses had been written in red ink next to certain names. He looked closer. Eight of the twenty-three were marked with a cross. His heart began to pound. Two of them were names he knew very well: Arkadi Slobodin and Stepan Dragunsky. But that wasn't all. The little crosses had clearly been made with a felt-tipped pen. They couldn't date back thirty years. In fact, they'd been made very recently.

Outside, it was raining—an irritating, monotonous rain compared to the deluge of the day before. Saunders cast a glum look down the street.

"There's nothing more depressing than Vienna in bad weather," he said to Schneider. "This kind of rain is O.K. for Paris; it fits in with the landscape, the people, the atmosphere. Here, it's no good."

Schneider tried to smile.

Suddenly Saunders stopped and felt his pockets. "Damn

it, I left my notebook down there. It must be on the table. Will you wait for me for a second?"

"I'll go with you," Schneider offered.

"No, no, don't bother."

He spun around and ran towards the gloomy entrance of the old Rathaus. Schneider shrugged and found shelter against the building's façade.

Saunders was back in a few minutes. "I found it. What do we do now?"

"I suggest we return to my house," Schneider said. "We'll see what we can find on Block 13 in my files. There might be something interesting." He didn't sound very optimistic.

"Good idea." Saunders was suddenly gay. "But why don't we have a drink first? It's a long time since I was at the Hohenzollern."

Schneider looked pointedly at his watch. "I'm terribly afraid that..."

"Please, Egon, for my sake." Saunders knew how to turn on the charm when necessary. Schneider gave in with an indulgent smile.

Saunders joked and chatted up to the moment when the old maître d'hôtel with his starched jacket and solemn face brought them the picturesque bottle of Viennese wine in its wrought-iron cradle. He filled each glass with the delicate perfumed Riesling.

Schneider said *"Prosit"*, and lifted his glass.

Saunders did not reply. All signs of good humour had gone from his face. He looked straight into Schneider's eyes.

"What's the matter?" Schneider asked him. "Is something wrong?"

Saunders sighed. He was silent for a moment, then burst out: "O.K., Egon. For Christ's sake, stop the nonsense and tell me what's going on."

Schneider winced as if he'd been slapped. He turned pale and put down his glass.

"What are you talking about? What nonsense?" His voice shook with indignation.

"Oh, come on! Here I am, in a mad race against time, trying to prevent a disaster, with you doing nothing but put spokes in my wheels, and now you have the gall to pretend

you're outraged. Tell me the truth. That's all I ask." Out of
the corner of his eye, Saunders could see people turning to
listen. He tried to pull himself together, took a deep breath
and without looking at Schneider, said in a calm voice: "I
thought we were friends. I asked you to help me with something extremely important. You haven't told me half what
you know. Why not?"

Schneider didn't answer.

Saunders looked at him and continued calmly: "When I
arrived at your place yesterday, you greeted me like a friend.
Then the moment I mentioned the two Russians at Dachau,
you turned very strange. You knew who they were, you even
knew their names and the whole history of Block 13. Why
did you hide it from me?"

"What makes you think I knew all this?"

"What? I only had to look at your face and see how nervous
you were. You asked me: 'Is this really such a very serious
matter?' That was an uneasy conscience talking. Down in
the Rathaus basement, where you said nobody'd been for a
long time, you went straight to the files where the reports
on Dragunsky and Slobodin were and the whole dossier on
Block 13. It didn't take you five minutes. Which means
you knew the contents, you'd seen them recently. The custodian said the basement had been electrified because you
used the archives so often now. Why, Herr Schneider? And
with whom?"

Schneider was on the defensive: "I had a visit three
months ago from three members of the Organisation of Former Internees whose main offices are in Berne, Switzerland.
They said they wanted to make a list of all the Dachau and
Buchenwald survivors. I placed my archives at their disposal
for about a week, as I've done for many other such groups.
Was there anything wrong with that?'

"Who else did you take down to the basement?"

"What is this? A police interrogation?" Schneider was
angrier than Saunders had ever seen him. "Who else do you
think I took down?"

"I'll tell you who." Saunders took his notebook out of his
pocket. "Actually, I hadn't left my notebook in the basement.
I asked you to wait only so that I could ask the custodian a

74

few questions. A couple of hundred schillings loosened his tongue.

"Two months ago, you went to the archives with a young man—French or Belgian, he thought. You went twice, on two successive days. Would you like me to describe the young man? Medium tall, brown hair, thin, wearing a polo-necked shirt under a jacket and a light blue raincoat. You spoke French together. You want more, Herr Schneider?"

The Austrian looked down. He didn't speak for a long moment. Finally he met Saunders' gaze and sighed. There was a hint of the old warmth in his eyes.

"All right. I probably deserved this stupid scene. I forgot I was dealing with an old fox in the secret service."

Saunders said nothing.

"It's true," Schneider went on. "Everything you say is true. I knew all about it: Block 13, your Russians. Yes, I was in the basement not long ago. I said nothing because I was afraid I'd been careless or I might hurt a young man who trusted me and whom I trusted."

"Who is he?"

"I'll tell you the whole thing from the beginning. About two months ago, I received a telephone call from a man who works for Editions Fontenoy in Paris. Quite young, around thirty years old. He's a reader for Fontenoy and has specialised in the history of the Nazi holocaust, the Résistance, the Second World War. He had already visited me several times to ask my advice on manuscripts. Not from the literary point of view, of course. He simply wanted to check the books' authenticity and find out if they revealed anything new."

"Documentary things?"

"Yes. Contemporary history. He wasn't interested in novels. Then he called me a few days ago. He was very excited. He said he wanted to come to Vienna to check on certain details concerning Dachau. He said he had just received an extraordinary manuscript to which he attached the greatest importance. It was going to be published by Editions Fontenoy towards the end of September.

"He arrived the next day. He told me he had left the manuscript in Paris but he'd made notes on the most important details and wanted to check certain facts about Block

75

13 at Dachau and what happened during the years 1944 and 1945. He had a list of sixteen names: Joakim Müller, the S.S. officer in charge of the block, and fifteen inmates. Dragunsky and Slobodin were among them. We went to the archives together and found the file with the reports. He particularly wanted to know where these people were now—what had happened to them. I explained that my archives only went up to 1946, but he might be able to find their current addresses at the Zentralstelle in Ludwigsburg. You know the place. They have up-to-date lists of all known survivors so that, if necessary, they can call on them for testimony. In fact, they have copies of all my own lists.

"Following my advice, the young man went to Ludwigsburg and called me after a few days. He told me he had succeeded in finding the addresses of almost all the men he was interested in. Of the fifteen former prisoners, several had died but he had found all the others with one exception: Slobodin. He asked me to try to find Joakim Müller's address also—he had apparently disappeared after the war. I don't think he has a chance of finding him, but all the same I got in touch with all the organisations I work with. Nothing has been found so far.

"That is the story. When you barged into my study in the middle of the night with your air of high drama, the dangers to world peace and all that—then gave me the names of those two Russians at Dachau—I have to admit I was scared. I thought maybe this boy and I had unintentionally provoked some international crisis. Or was it a simple coincidence? You know, I feel great sympathy for this young man. He's an honest, committed boy and it's hard to think of him mixed up in a conspiracy. That is why I decided to check with him before I told you all I knew, to find out if he was involved in this affair of yours, or if it was pure coincidence. When you left last night, I telephoned him in Paris but there was no answer. I thought I might telephone Editions Fontenoy today ..."

"No, don't do anything." Saunders grasped his friend's arm. "Please believe me. I understand exactly how you feel and I'm sorry I talked the way I did. I didn't mean to sound as if I suspected you. But please don't telephone him. I don't think he did anything wrong and I'm sure he acted in good faith when he came to see you, just as you did when you helped him. But I repeat: this is a matter of great importance. Let me handle it my way. I'll go to Ludwigsburg today myself, and I'll probably be in Paris tomorrow night. I have only one more thing to ask you: his name."

Schneider gave him a long look. Then he slumped in his chair and said with an air of resignation: "His name is Jean-Marc Luçot."

6

Jeremy Lansing was waiting for him at the airport in Stuttgart. Saunders didn't like Lansing and knew the feeling was mutual. Lansing was short and fat with a moon-face and pig eyes, and he had been the C.I.A. chief for Southern Germany—meaning Stuttgart, Munich and Nuremberg for several years. Outwardly, he was a respectable supplier of produce to the American bases in the region, but Gehlen's operators knew perfectly well who he really was and the true nature of his activities. It would have been impossible to hide them from the Germans, and anyway there was no reason to. The United States and West Germany worked closely together in the battle against Communist espionage. The Gehlen ring in the U.S.S.R. was still run by the agents that the wily old general had appointed during World War II. He had managed to keep control over them and was able to place them at the West's disposal when the cold war broke out.

The fact that the German security forces knew Lansing's identity didn't bother the C.I.A. at all. He hadn't been assigned a secret mission for a long time. He was nothing more than an antenna, a liaison man for the transmission of documents, information, funds and equipment to agents who were working, as often as not, hand in glove with the Germans. When a really secret mission came up, the C.I.A. used a totally different network. Lansing knew it existed but he didn't know who was in it.

Saunders wasn't surprised to find Lansing at the airport. It was his sort of activity.

78

"Welcome to sunny Deutschland," Lansing said with forced gaiety. In spite of the heat, he wore a hat and coat which made him look all the more stolid.

"Hello, Lansing," Saunders said without enthusiasm. He knew all about Lansing's extraordinary exploits during World War II, his courage and *sang froid*, but he left Saunders cold. And he knew Lansing didn't like him any better, calling him "Playboy 007", "Papillon" and "Superman" behind his back. Their relationship had always been distant, which suited them well enough.

Lansing took a sealed envelope from his inside pocket and handed it to Saunders. "This is for you. You'll find five hundred marks in it, some cables from Washington and the receipt for a reservation at the Europäischer Hof in Ludwigsburg. Do you want to check it out?"

"No," Saunders said. "I trust you."

Lansing shrugged. "They told me to rent you a car. Here are the keys. The licence number is on the key-ring. You'll find the car in the airport parking lot, third row, first on your left. The registration is in the glove compartment. I also left a map on the seat with the route to Ludwigsburg marked on it."

"I'll make out," Saunders said.

Lansing couldn't hold back. "They're really spoiling you in Washington. Sullivan insisted I find you a Mercedes 'Spider' 350. Nothing else would do."

"You don't think I deserve it?" Saunders asked with sarcasm. "After all, aren't I the boss's darling? By the way, what kind of car do you have?"

Lansing ignored the jibe. "If you need to send any wires, just call me. I put my calling card and telephone number in your envelope. All you have to do is invite me for a drink. I'll come, or send somebody else. When do you leave?"

"Probably tomorrow."

"For . . . ?"

"Paris."

"Right. That's what Washington told me. I suppose you want to leave in the morning?" Saunders nodded. "There are four morning flights to Paris. I made two reservations for you, one on Lufthansa at ten thirty and another on Air France at eleven ten. You'll find the reservations in your name at the information desk in the main hall. All they need is to be stamped by the airline. Leave the car keys at the information desk and I'll take care of the rest."

"You've thought of everything, haven't you?"

Lansing gave him a suspicious look, not sure whether Saunders was being sincere or trying for another thrust in their endless duel. "That's all, I think."

"Thanks a lot, Lansing. I hope I don't need to call you from Ludwigsburg."

Lansing gave him a limp hand. "Goodbye. And don't forget to put in a good word for me in Washington. You sleep better nights when you know you have a friend at the top."

Saunders watched the heavy silhouette disappear into the crowd. He looked at his watch: two fifteen p.m. He just had time for a quick drink and a glance at the telegrams. It couldn't take more than an hour and a half to get to Ludwigsburg; the "Spider" could easily do ninety on the Autobahn. He smiled, remembering Lansing's envy over the car. But Lansing was right. The fact that Sullivan had taken the trouble to cable his Stuttgart representative to provide him, Saunders, with his favourite car was a sure sign that he was being given the V.I.P. treatment. It had taken only forty-eight hours to make him a *persona* very *grata* in the big building on the far side of the Potomac.

Saunders decoded the seemingly innocent "commercial" wires with the help of the personal code Sullivan had given him before he left. Each telegram had been written out, then the "sensitive" expressions or words had been replaced by words from a list made up for this particular mission, a list which only Saunders, Sullivan and Richards had. For example, "killer" was replaced by "client", Slobodin and Dragunsky had become, respectively, "calculating machine" and "electronic camera". Dachau was "European warehouse". A sentence like: "The killer knew that Slobodin and Dragunsky had been together at Dachau" became "Client aware calculating machine and electronic camera both in European warehouse."

These "commercial" telegrams were coded by the State

Department and sent to agents via the various U.S. embassies or commercial representatives in the major European cities. Saunders' wires had been received in Stuttgart where they were decoded and then converted again into innocent business telegrams. He in turn had to reinterpret them according to his own list.

Saunders had learned from experience that the safest place to conduct secret business was in a public place, and the more crowded the better. So he sat down at a table in the middle of the small airport café, ordered a large stein of beer and opened and decoded Lansing's envelope. Richards' wire was brief and exuberant: "Congratulations on Vienna success. You seem on right track. President very satisfied. Russians know. Keep it up. Hal."

Jim Sullivan's was more functional: "In answer to your 28/8. Preliminary investigation Jean-Marc Luçot in our records negative, repeat negative. Preliminary investigation on above by Paris representative, negative, repeat negative. Wire Paris give urgent priority to further investigation of Luçot and prepare report for your arrival Paris 30/8. Reports on Dachau Block 13 by Eighth Division Regiments 824 and 743, nothing new. All investigations of Dragunsky and Slobodin activities pertaining to espionage, crime, subversion, negative. New York investigation suspended because of impasse; Soviet secret service have nothing on Slobodin, nor Dragunsky before desertion. Nothing new on Ponomarev murder. Soviets waiting as promised but growing signs of nervousness in Red Army circles. Propose you concentrate on Zentralstelle Ludwigsburg and Luçot Paris. Send news of new developments immediately. All European stations at your service. Good luck. End. Jim."

Saunders found the silvery "Spider" without any trouble. He felt a wonderful sense of physical well-being as he sank into the soft black leather seat. The engine was tuned to perfection and the gear shift responded to the lightest touch of his fingers. He addressed a few baleful thoughts to the inventor of the automatic shift, bore down on the accelerator and, with an arrogant whine of the tires, the car headed for the access road to the Autobahn.

Absentmindedly he noticed a big black Mercedes in his

rear view mirror leaving the parking lot behind him. Then he turned his attention to the heavy traffic on the access road. Giving the "Spider" its head, he darted between two cars and roared full speed onto the Autobahn.

As he drove, he tried to arrange his thoughts for a preliminary report on his investigation. He could see no reason not to believe Schneider's story. He knew the man was honest. If Schneider had hidden certain things from him at the beginning, it was only because he didn't want to hurt the young Frenchman by raising false suspicions. Saunders tried to figure out Jean-Marc's role in the affair. At most, someone was using him. The idea that Luçot could be a conscious member of the conspiracy seemed very unlikely. In the first place, his enquiries at Schneider's sounded perfectly innocent; his job as a reader for Editions Fontenoy and the fact that he specialised in books about concentration camps was surely enough to justify his trips to Vienna and Ludwigsburg. And the reasons for his recent visit to Schneider also seemed perfectly plausible. Furthermore it would be very odd that a man directly involved in a conspiracy would leave such obvious traces; an apprentice detective could have picked up the scent in a few hours. Much more logical was the possibility that Luçot was being manipulated by the men who had thought up and executed the murders. Perhaps they had seen to it that he received a certain manuscript, into which they had slipped a few details that needed verification which Luçot would provide in the course of his work. Or maybe it was the other way around: they had made use of Luçot only after he had obtained the information for his own work. It was also possible that the manuscript was pure invention and that Luçot had lied to Schneider; couldn't friends, or even strangers who knew of Luçot's connection with groups doing research on World War II have offered to pay him for doing a little file snooping? Luçot needn't have any idea what lay behind their requests. But what was the motive of those who were using him? What was the secret of Block 13 at Dachau? Money? Revenge? Espionage? More and more, he was convinced that Paris held the key to his mission. He was sure of it: either Luçot or the manuscript or maybe both would solve the mystery.

When he arrived in Ludwigsburg, Saunders went straight to the Zentralstelle. He parked his car in the ugly square in front of the old prison that now served as the research centre on Nazi criminals, and walked briskly to the main entrance. The guard in the lobby must have recognised him for he let him go right past without asking for identification. Saunders climbed to the third floor, checked the directory for the archives rooms, and started down the endless corridor. It was completely deserted; not a sound from behind the dozens of closed doors—only his footsteps echoing between bare walls. There was something sinister in the heavy silence: the building was dead, like the thousands of names in the countless files and drawers locked behind those doors.

He stopped in front of the door marked 371, knocked and went in. "Herr Stoff?"

A young girl with dark brown hair and black eyes was sitting at a desk piled high with clippings. She looked at him with surprise.

"Herr Stoff isn't here." Her voice was melodious and warm, clearly out of place in this morgue. "He is on vacation and won't be back until September 15th. But perhaps I can help you? I'm Inge Knutte, his assistant." As she spoke, she kept on inserting clippings into various large envelopes. She had a practised hand. "I'm afraid you'll have to come back tomorrow. I was just finishing up when you came in. During the summer, we work only until two in the afternoon. Could you tell me what you are here for?"

In these few seconds, Saunders completely lost his assurance. What could he say to this girl? It never occurred to him that Rudy Stoff ever took a vacation. Every time he had been to the Zentralstelle, Rudy Stoff had been there at his desk, his white hair carefully combed, solemnly dressed in immaculate white shirt, stiff collar and bow tie. Stoff had always seemed inseparable from his office, as if he were part of the furniture. He knew Saunders well and knew everything about his functions. After the war and Stoff's return from a long political exile in Sweden, U.S. Intelligence had found him useful in its search for Nazi war criminals. He subsequently joined the German government and when the Zentralstelle was established, he naturally gravitated to it as archive director. His relations with the Americans had remained close and he often collaborated with their agents when they needed information. It had never dawned on Saunders that he might not find him in Ludwigsburg, and yet here he was, faced with this inquisitive girl and forced to improvise on the spur of the moment.

"It's rather difficult to explain," he said with a diffident smile, trying to gain time. "Have you been working here long?"

She hesitated. "Yes, fairly long. I've been here since January."

"That's why I haven't seen you before. I used to come often, but it's been a year now. My name is Jeff Saunders."

She bowed her head with a hint of mockery.

"I work for the publishing house of Ruben and Taylor in New York. We do quite a few books on the Second World War, many of them dealing with Nazi crimes, the concentration camps or some aspect of the 'final solution' to the Jewish question. So we have to check the authenticity of the stories—names, details, that sort of thing. If we're not careful, we run the risk of libel suits and other legal complications. That's what brings me here from time to time."

"Yes, I see." Her tone was very solemn.

She had finished her work, tidied her desk, taken her bag from one of the drawers and was now heading for the door with Saunders tagging after. Her brightly coloured dress swished around her pretty legs.

"Why is everything so quiet? Is nobody here?"

She shook her head. "Nobody. They have all gone home. But go on. You were telling me...?"

He tried to hide his growing irritation. The wild chase to Ludwigsburg had been useless; he had wasted twenty-four precious hours because of the damn summer schedule imposed by some damn union. Not to mention Stoff's absence. But the most irritating thing of all was not being able to cope with this handsome, tantalising girl.

"Where was I? Oh yes. We recently received a very interesting manuscript that deals with ... with Dachau. It was sent to us by Editions Fontenoy in Paris. They have already

84

researched the book and confirmed its accuracy, but since I was in Europe for the coming Frankfurt Book Fair, and the material in the book is of a highly ... how shall I put it? ... sensitive nature, I thought I would like to check it myself."

They had arrived at the elevator.

"Of course," the girl said smiling. "Now I know what you are referring to. A representative of Editions Fontenoy was here less than a month ago. A very nice young man, though a little strange. You know the type—very quiet, very secretive. We did a lot of work for him."

Saunders barely managed to control his excitement. "Is that so? Are you quite sure it's the same manuscript?"

"I think so. What was it called ... *Letters in Blood*, isn't that it? The Frenchman from Fontenoy—I think his name was Duçot, no, Luçot—told us the manuscript was written with blood, the author's own blood. I couldn't sleep nights after I heard that. It's horrible."

They were now in the courtyard, hot in the afternoon sun. "Is that the manuscript you've come about?" she asked again.

"Yes," he said quickly, "although the American version will probably have another title."

No reaction.

He continued flatly: "I don't understand why Fontenoy thought it needed more checking. All the research had been done some time ago."

"I think they were looking for some of the people mentioned in the manuscript—the people in Block 13. They hadn't been able to get their addresses, and they weren't even sure they were still alive."

"Did they turn up anything?"

"We didn't do too badly," she said with some pride. "I did the work myself. We got in touch with the International Red Cross in Geneva and with several refugee groups and were able to trace most of the people mentioned. You know," her eyes grew bright, "I spent a whole day looking through the archives and I even discovered a photograph of the block with the Nazi officer in charge—somebody named Müller. You know how people like that enjoy being photographed with their victims."

Saunders turned to the girl. "Listen, can I ask you a personal favour? I didn't know you closed so early, and I promised to phone my boss in New York with the results of my research. Since you know all about this business, couldn't you show me the file now? Or, so that I don't hold you up, I could take the file, have the documents I need photocopied and return the whole thing tomorrow morning."

She was very firm. "No, I can't do it. We are forbidden to loan the files without the director's authorisation. A few months ago, we were visited by some members of an organisation of camp survivors—they came from Switzerland, I think —and I was naïve enough to let them have all our Dachau files and photographs to copy. I got into terrible hot water. It's true they returned everything in three days, but I was almost fired."

"Why? What was so bad about that?" Saunders asked.

"According to the directors of the Zentralstelle, there are thousands of Nazis who are very interested in our archives. All kinds of people who want to have their past forgotten, who fear we may have incriminating documents. They'd give a small fortune to have any evidence against them destroyed and might well try to pass as researchers or representatives of a publishing house in order to steal the documents."

"You mean me?" Saunders said with a smile.

She laughed. "No, no. But you have to admit it makes sense. We were not in the habit of cross-questioning the people who came here, or making identity checks. So anybody who really wanted to had no trouble getting at the documents he was interested in. That's why we recently doubled security measures in the archives rooms."

"So, what am I going to do?" Saunders asked with a sigh.

"Wait until tomorrow. It won't take half an hour to find everything you want. All the documents about Dachau that we collected for Luçot are together in one place. I have the keys to the archives and I give you my word that I will be here at eight thirty tomorrow morning. Are you planning to stay long?"

Saunders shook his head. "Not more than twenty-four hours." But his thoughts were elsewhere: to have to wait until tomorrow morning, losing yet another day, was a luxury he couldn't afford. He had already lost too much time in

86

Miami and Vienna. He absolutely had to get those documents that night. But how? There wasn't a soul left at the Zentralstelle. Everything was locked up. Stoff was gone and the only one who could help him was this ravishing and stubborn girl he would love to have met in another place, under different circumstances. Now he'd have to make a deliberate attempt to seduce her. There were times in the past when he would have felt no scruples about the prospect, but he had the feeling this girl was something special.

A little shamefaced, he produced another deep sigh and what he hoped was an irresistible smile. "Am I going to be left here alone until tomorrow morning, lost and abandoned in a strange town?"

Inge Knutte laughed. "Oh ho! So the Big Bad Wolf has finally noticed Little Red Riding Hood. But I'd better warn you that I understand you very well. This game amuses you?" No answer from Saunders. "All right then, if you insist, I will tell you that you don't seem at all lost to me. And as for your loneliness, you look like the kind of man who won't stay lonely for very long."

His smile broadened: "Yes, but it's not every day that I meet..."

"Come on, drop it." Her warm smile belied her sharp tone. "I know exactly what you're going to say: you're going to launch into a classic Don Juan monologue and tell me that it isn't every day you meet anyone as beautiful, as understanding, as intelligent as I, that you thank your lucky stars that old Rudy Stoff wasn't here, that we absolutely must get to know each other better, and so why can't we have dinner together tonight? That's it, isn't it?"

Saunders raised his arms in a gesture of mock helplessness. "You win. But now that you've brought it up, why don't we have dinner tonight?"

She was serious again and looked him straight in the eye.

"Look, I'm not going to say 'But I don't know you, etc...' That would be stupid. I would like to have dinner with you tonight, but you and I know very well what happens after dinner with a man like you. I don't like this kind of one-night stand. How do you say it in America? It would be bad for my psychic equilibrium."

87

She took a deep breath and tried to smile. "So, until tomorrow morning at eight thirty. And that's final. But if you should ever come back, and I'm free and you have more time, I promise we'll have our dinner, dessert included."

She blushed and rushed down the stone steps, leaving behind a very bewildered and frustrated man.

It was eleven forty-three when the television announcer signed off for the night. Jeff Saunders stretched in his chair, blinked his eyes and yawned. He placed his half-empty glass of Scotch on the floor, got to his feet, turned off the set and opened his suitcase. From a kit he took out a bunch of keys, a small set of burglar's tools, a flash light and a pair of brass knuckles, all of which he stuffed into his various pockets. Everything he had on was black: jacket, turtleneck shirt, trousers, and his light weight moccasins with the soft rubber soles. He took a last look at his watch before wedging it into a pocket: the luminous dial said eleven fifty-six. He was fairly certain the guard at the Zentralstelle would be asleep, now that television was over for the night. Saunders was sure there would be only one guard and that he wouldn't be the kind who made regular patrols during the night. For all that there were sensational documents in its files, it was not a military installation and, logically, one guard would be enough. Despite Inge Knutte's story about the strengthening of security measures, he was sure that they'd done nothing more than install some kind of alarm system, controlled from the guard's post which would set off bells in the various corners of the building. If this were so, forcing an entry into the archives room wouldn't be too difficult. He'd done much trickier things before. But it did seem a little ridiculous to have to use such methods when he had walked through the front door on so many occasions. And not because he wanted some secret document, but only to gain a little time so that he could make the ten-thirty plane for Paris the next morning.

He picked up the phone. "I'm going to bed now," he said to the sleepy switchboard girl. "Don't put through any more telephone calls, and please call me at six a.m."

She repeated mechanically: "Room 301. Call for six a.m. Yes, sir. Good night, sir."

He put out the lights, went out, locked the door and hung the "Please don't disturb" sign on the knob. Instead of using the elevator, he walked down the stairs. Once on the ground floor, he headed for the service entrance which opened onto the parking lot. He threaded his way between the cars and took the first little street to the left where he had left the "Spider".

He parked the car in a deserted street a few hundred yards from the Zentralstelle and walked up to the wall that surrounded what had once been the Ludwigsburg prison. He took his watch out of his pocket: twelve twenty-five a.m.

Climbing the wall and running across the courtyard was easy. He hugged the wall until he reached the east wing of the old prison. This section was empty except for the ground floor which had been modernised and made into the employees' cafeteria. He had chosen this spot for his entry, remembering that the cafeteria was connected with the offices by a long corridor and that it had only a simple wooden door. It was unlikely that the cafeteria windows and the wooden door would be wired.

He heard the sound of a car passing slowly on the other side of the wall, flattened himself against it and waited. When the car had gone, he grabbed onto one of the stone window-sills, hoisted himself up and once securely perched there, flicked on his flashlight to examine the window frame. He smiled, remembering his first lesson in house-breaking at the special school for secret agents. He'd been right: there was no sign of wiring. He took a small pair of pliers, a screwdriver and two thin strips of black steel with sharpened ends. For two minutes he pried and tugged, then, his foot anchored against the sill, he pressed gently on the window. The two sides opened with a small creaking noise and he leapt in.

He slid silently between the metal tables of the cafeteria, opened the wooden door with one of his pass keys and arrived in the Zentralstelle proper, still and dark as the grave. Climbing to the third floor, he stopped in front of the main door leading into the archives room. Instinct told him to be careful here. He put his tools on the floor and crawled around in search of the alarm system.

He almost missed the electronic eye. It was camouflaged

as an innocent screw in the door hinge. Its invisible ray crossed the threshold of the door diagonally, hitting a tiny crack in the door frame.

It took him over fifteen minutes to find the third-floor fuse box, in particular the fuse for the security system which was hidden in a corner some distance from the other fuses. It was one thirty-two a.m. by the time he finally got into the archives room.

He checked the shutters and heavy draperies to make certain the room was sealed. Using only his flashlight, he started a methodical inspection of each cabinet. The archives were endless: dozens of metal filing cabinets, wooden shelves filled with books and documents, long steel card files and many thousands of dossiers stacked on interminable rows of shelves. He would have drowned in this ocean of paper were it not for his previous experience at the Zentralstelle, his knowledge of the director's methods and the German obsession with organisation and order. Even so, it was past two a.m. when he finally found the current dossier on Dachau.

It was a slim file. Almost immediately, he came upon the brown folder with "Jean-Marc Luçot; Fontenoy; Letters in Blood" written in large block letters. The first document was the regulation form describing the nature of the quest:

Ludwigsburg, May 12th
Name: Jean-Marc Luçot
Profession: Reader for Editions Fontenoy,
     75, rue Monsieur-le-Prince, Paris VI
Nature of Request: Aid in locating some of the persons mentioned in the manuscript *Letters in Blood* by Georges Brisseau, discovered in a hiding place at Dachau concentration camp. Manuscript to be published in the autumn by Editions Fontenoy.
Material wanted: Current addresses of the following survivors of Block 13 at Dachau:
 1. Michel Talbot (French)
 2. Marc Brajinski (Polish)
 3. Arkadi Slobodin (Russian)
 4. Lev Jourbin (Russian Jew)
 5. Stepan Dragunsky (Russian)

6. Johann Cyrankiewitz (Polish)
7. Hendrik Van Velden (Dutch)
8. Robert Mischo (Belgian)

I should also like to know the whereabouts of war-criminal S.S. Sturmführer Joakim Müller, guard in charge of Block 13.

Signed:	Received by:
Jean-Marc Luçot	Inge Knutte

Saunders examined the list very carefully. He took out the documents he had "borrowed" from Schneider's Rathaus basement and compared the two lists. The names of the eight people Luçot was enquiring after here were the same as those marked with a red cross on the Vienna list.

Then he leafed through the other documents in the file: copies of letters to the International Red Cross and to various groups of refugees in Vienna, Brussels, Warsaw, Berne and Paris. There was a letter to "Yad Vachem"—a memorial in Jerusalem to the Jewish victims of Nazism—and a memo to Zentralstelle employees asking them to keep an eye out for any references to the above names during the course of their work. Saunders riffled through with growing impatience until he came to the replies.

On a piece of pink paper with *Zentralstelle* at the top, someone had written "For inside use only: No information on Joakim Müller. Sought for war crimes: extensive extermination of internees, torture, direct responsibility for the death of about 800 prisoners at Dachau. Assume he is still alive but no idea where."

A letter from the International Federation of Former Deportees in Brussels reported that Hendrik Van Velden, of 127 Herrengracht Street in Amsterdam, died on March 12th, 1968, and that Robert Mischo of 17, rue de la Loi in Liège, died in the municipal hospital on July 12th, 1961.

There were letters from different refugee groups giving information on several of the names, then finally he came to the Zentralstelle's answer to Jean-Marc Luçot:

Ludwigsburg, June 7th
Dear Mr. Luçot:
In response to your request of May 12th, we contacted

91

the various international organisations who deal with survivors of concentration camps. On the basis of their answers, we are able to give you the following information:

1. Michel Talbot lives in France. He is the correspondent on aeronautical affairs for *Le Courrier de Lyon*. His address is 145, Avenue General de Gaulle, Villefranche.

2. Marc Brajinski left Crakow and moved to South Africa in 1951. He lives at 72 Lord Kitchener Avenue in Capetown.

3. Lev Jourbin emigrated to Israel. He lives at 18 Bialik Street in Ashkelon.

4. Johann Cyrankiewitz lives at 122 Franziskanska St., Lodz, Poland.

5. Hendrik Van Velden died in Amsterdam in 1968.

6. Robert Mischo died in Liège in 1961.

7. We are unable to find an address for Stepan Dragunsky. The groups we contacted have lost all trace of him. He is thought to have emigrated to the United States and to be living in Miami, Florida. He broke off all relations with refugee organisations and has apparently changed his name to Steven Dragner. We suggest you get in touch with the local authorities, or check with the local telephone directory.

8. We have no information on Arkadi Slobodin.

9. We have no information on S.S. Sturmführer Joakim Müller, though we believe that he is still alive. However, we have been fortunate in finding a document that may be useful to you. It is a print of a photograph of Joakim Müller taken with a group of prisoners in Block 13 at Dachau. The photograph is dated January 1945. It is probable that some of the prisoners you mentioned are in it. Unfortunately we have been unable to identify them for we have no pictures of the individual prisoners.

I am enclosing a copy of the photograph.

Sincerely yours,
Inge Knutte
p/ Rudy Stoff, Director of the Central Archives.

Saunders examined the picture attached to the letter. The original must be in the Dachau Archives, he thought. They must have made two copies, one for Luçot and one for the Zentralstelle-Luçot correspondence. There was Müller with his arrogant face and carefully pressed black uniform, and the fifteen prisoners, their tragic and terrified eyes staring into the camera.

Looking at the faces, his attention was immediately drawn to a tall thin man with a flat nose and prominent ears. His face was vaguely familiar. Of course: Dragunsky. For all the thirty years since Dachau, there was a definite resemblance between this man and the Dragner in the Miami police headquarters file.

Slobodin's face, however, was truly astonishing. It had remained practically unchanged during the course of a quarter century. The expression in this picture was exactly the same as the one he had seen on his passport. There was the calm assurance which the atrocities at Dachau had left untouched. "That's a Russian *mujik* for you," Saunders said to himself. "Tough as steel. It's what beat Napoleon at Moscow..."

He folded the documents, taking special care not to hurt the photograph, and tucked the lot into his jacket pocket. He was about to put the file back in its place when he had an idea. Taking a piece of paper from a near-by table, he wrote: "Dear Inge: I had to leave sooner than expected. But I'll come back for our dinner. Yours, Jeff Saunders."

He slipped the note into the folder, put the dossier back where he had found it and, pleased with his work, walked briskly to the door.

His hand was already on the knob when a muffled sound of footsteps reached his ears. He froze. The sound grew louder, slow, regular footsteps climbing the stairs, pausing, then resuming. He turned off his flashlight and flattened himself behind a large metal cabinet. The steps came nearer. Jeff waited in the dark, his heart pounding, almost certain it was the guard on his nightly rounds.

The steps approached the door to the archives, less than six feet from where he stood. Did the guard suspect something? Suddenly the steps stopped. Jeff thought he heard a smothered exclamation and the sound of something heavy

93

falling to the ground near the door. Then everything was silent again.

A few minutes passed. Slowly, Jeff moved towards the door and stopped. Not a sound anywhere in the vast building. Two more steps and he was at the door. He stopped again. He turned the knob with great care, opened the door and peered down the corridor. A curious sight met his eyes.

The guard was sitting on the floor a few feet away, his back propped against the wall. He was a fat old German, probably an army veteran, wearing a wrinkled blue uniform. A large flashlight and a walkie-talkie lay on the floor beside him.

A strange scene—the total silence, and the guard sitting there motionless. Saunders decided to take a chance. He tiptoed into the corridor and to the guard. He leaned over him; the old man was breathing heavily as if he were asleep. Gingerly, Jeff felt the back of his neck: a big bump had already begun to form.

Somebody—clearly an expert in such matters—had knocked him out with a single blow.

7

Most of the first class passengers on Lufthansa's Flight 462, destination Paris, were very correct, stolid German businessmen—pink-cheeked, not a hair out of place, and deadly dull. Jeff Saunders gave them a jaundiced look and leaned back in his seat with a deep sigh. He was pale, his face drawn and there were black circles under his blood-shot eyes. He needed sleep. He had barely closed an eye since his return to the hotel at dawn and the dash for the Stuttgart airport. As Jeremy Lansing promised, his ticket was waiting for him at the information desk. No problems with passport or customs either. The evening's activity at the Zentralstelle had not yet made the papers, though it seemed odd that the radio stations hadn't carried it by nine thirty when he surrendered the keys to the "Spider".

He sank into a gentle doze and woke up only when he heard the stewardess's discreet cough. She was holding a tray of assorted titbits running the gamut from "German caviar" —a cheap fake—to the real stuff from the Caspian Sea.

"Would you like some vodka, sir?"

He shook his head. From time to time, his French blood asserted itself. "A split of champagne, please." He watched with pleasure as the bubbling liquid flowed into his glass. But the pleasure vanished when he saw the bold headlines on the *New York Times* he picked up from a passing wagon.

"RED ARMY ON ALERT," and under it in smaller type: "Massive movement of Warsaw Pact tanks and artillery towards

95

German border. President convenes National Security Council for second time in twenty-four hours. U.S.S.R. hawks gain as consequence of Ponomarev murder."

In the article itself, each piece of information was more disquieting than the next:

Dependable sources in Moscow report today a growing impatience among Red Army leaders over United States delay in solving the murder of Foreign Minister Ponomarev. Army hawks maintain that the slowness of the investigation supports their thesis that the assassination was deliberately prepared at the highest level to remove from the political scene an obstacle to American foreign policy. The Red Army chiefs—headed by Generals Stolipin and Novikov—are of the opinion that the Americans have run into difficulties in finding a plausible explanation for the crime and have been drawing out the investigation to gain time.

At the Red Army's instigation, Soviet leaders have decided on a series of military measures: the entire Red Army has been placed on alert; all airports and rocket bases are on a war footing. Furthermore, C.I.A. listening posts along the Soviet border have picked up an unusual number of radio messages indicating that a growing number of fighter planes and bombers have begun engaging in war exercises. The C.I.A. has also succeeded in picking up messages sent to orbiting Russian satellites. These are believed to be instructions aimed at modifying the satellite orbits to enable them to photograph American installations.

Sizeable infantry, tank and artillery units are currently crossing Poland towards the German border; tank squadrons have taken up positions around Berlin. Since midnight, all access to West Berlin has been cut. Over the heated objections of the Western powers, Soviet and East German authorities have refused to explain the move or indicate when the blockade will be lifted.

Feverish preparations have also been noted at Soviet bases in Cuba, Egypt, Algeria and in the Indian Ocean. Twelve Soviet warships, six submarines and two supply ships passed through the Bosphorous into the Mediterranean this morning at dawn.

The *Times* Washington correspondent reported mounting efforts at the White House to preserve the peace.

Official sources indicate that the President has decided not to take parallel military counter-measures for the moment in order to underscore his desire for detente. There is grave anxiety at the White House, but there is also a determination to resolve the crisis in a spirit of mutual understanding. As for the murder of Ponomarev, the Federal authorities and the New York police continue to observe the most complete silence on the progress of the investigation. However, there is some indication that it has taken a new and unexpected turn in the past two days and results are anticipated in the very near future.

Saunders quickly scanned the inside pages until he reached the editorial columns. Under the heading "Surprise in Moscow", the well-known journalist Roy Jameson wrote:

It would be naïve to think that the murder of Minister Ponomarev is the real cause of the present crisis. At most, the crime was the spark that lit a fire which had long been smouldering in the Soviet Union. The West has been aware for some time of an intense struggle between the hardliners of the Red Army and the more moderate elements in the civilian government. It was no secret that the Army was advocating an intransigent Stalinist line and forcefully opposed any conference on disarmament. Still, it is clear that leaders and observers, both in the West and in the U.S.S.R. itself, underestimated the power of the hawks. The civilian chiefs in the Kremlin were astonished by the depth and extent of the military's influence, and have been forced to give in on several important points. No doubt the announcement of the alert, and the subsequent mobilisation, were undertaken with their consent; but this consent was certainly not given willingly, for it threatens to bring down the curtain on the Kremlin's efforts towards a rapprochement with the West. It seems probable that the government and party leaders in Moscow gave in to the military to avoid an internal crisis of unforeseeable consequences. The civilians may still be in control, and if the mystery of Ponomarev's murder is solved within the next few days, and if—as we have been led to believe—it was not a political assassination, the Kremlin may come out of this crisis with renewed strength and the power to impose its will on the Army. On the other hand, if the investigation continues to stall, the hawks—who seemed surprised themselves at the extent of their influence—may be lured into taking ill-considered measures and tempted to seize full power.

It was the last sentence that riveted Saunders' attention: "As a result of this unusual series of events, the peace of the world may well depend on a speedy solution to the murder. Every hour that passes threatens to be fatal."

A hostess was waiting for him at the end of the ramp at Orly. "Monsieur Saunders? I've been asked to take you to the T.W.A. counter in the transit area to check your connecting flight. Will you follow me, please? Thank you."

He was experienced enough not to show surprise over this "connecting flight" that had been arranged for him, so he dutifully followed the hostess through a series of lounges to the T.W.A. counter.

"Monsieur Saunders from Washington," the hostess informed the T.W.A. employee and left.

"Your passport, please, Mr. Saunders."

He took his passport from the inside pocket of his jacket. The employee examined the photograph, glancing at him with studied indifference, and handed it back. Then she opened a drawer and took out a small plastic envelope with his name on it.

"Here is your ticket and all the details of your connecting flight. Unfortunately, there is a two hour delay on the Hong Kong flight."

Saunders took the envelope, found a corner in the lounge and opened it. It did indeed contain an aeroplane ticket, but there was no destination indicated, no flight number, not even his name. He examined the several coupons; stapled to the last one he found a typewritten note: "Call immediately 425-71-20, System F." What was this? Since when had such precautions been necessary in a friendly capital like Paris? The moment the T.W.A. clerk had mentioned the Hong Kong flight he knew that his bosses had invented this story in order to avoid meeting him in person. But why? Why should personal contact be dangerous here?

He bought some telephone tokens at a tobacco kiosk and shut himself in a phone booth. "System F" was very simple. All it required was that he modify the sequence of numbers in the note by inverting each second number starting from the right, then inverting the whole. The result was 207-12-54.

He heard the phone ring at the other end. The receiver was picked up and a monotone voice said: "Are you on a clean line?"

"Yes."

"System F. Your number."

It took him almost a minute to get the number of his phone in code and spell it out to the anonymous listener.

"System F. Your personal number."

That he knew by heart.

"Hang up. We will call you right back."

Saunders hung up, irritated. This thriller nonsense gave him a pain. A large man sweating profusely appeared outside the booth, glaring impatiently at him as he mopped his forehead.

The telephone rang.

"Yes."

"System F. Your number."

He repeated his number in code.

"The line is clean. We can use it safely for two minutes and twenty seconds. I've been asked to give you the following instructions. Do you remember where you stayed the last time you were here?"

"Yes."

"They are expecting you. Use ordinary means of transportation. Further instructions and a car will be waiting for you there."

"All right."

"I've also been asked to tell you"—for a second, the voice had a touch of humanity—"that it was not possible to find you a Mercedes 'Spider' in all of Paris. I hope you know what that means. I don't."

He hung up. In the taxi that took him to the Orly Hilton, his irritation at the childish cops-and-robbers game melted as he thought of the man's confusion over the Mercedes "Spider".

The Orly Hilton gave him a warm welcome. "Yes, Monsieur Saunders, we received your telegram. We have reserved room 712 for you."

Room 712 was no room; it was a suite. The porter dropped his bags in the first room and vanished before Saunders had a chance to tip him. He opened the door to the second room and stopped in astonishment.

Standing at a small bar near the window, Hal Richards was pouring Scotch into two glasses. Without looking up, Richards said: "How much ice, Jeff?"

Saunders took a deep breath, pulled a metal box out of his pocket, extracted one of his interminable panatellas and lit it. Trying to match his boss's detachment, he said: "Two cubes, please."

He took the glass from Richards' hand and sank into an ugly modern chair.

"What have I done to deserve the attention of the big boss?"

Richards ignored the sarcasm.

"I happened to be passing through and I thought it would be nice to stop and have a drink with you." His smile was a little calculating.

"That stupid game at the airport was just so that you could say hello to me?"

"Well, not exactly."

Richards walked over to the window, pulled the curtains aside and absentmindedly watched the cars file down the Autoroute du Sud and disappear in the tunnel under the airport. "I knew you'd think it was all pretty silly. After all, we're in Paris, aren't we? But that's just it: we're in Paris. No other city in the world has so many of Chairman Mao's agents sniffing around. One look at their gigantic embassy on Avenue Montaigne will tell you it's not there just to further cultural ties with our rotting Western civilisation. If there's anyone who's interested in seeing that the investigation of Ponomarev's murder comes to nothing, it's the Chinese. Not to mention Russian military intelligence which has been very active in Paris lately. According to information that has come my way—although it's not yet confirmed—they're meddling in this business too. The other Soviet services may be ready to trust us, but not the G.R.U. They're on another tack. That's why I didn't want anybody to see us together or start shadowing you. I want to avoid their having the slightest suspicion that you're involved in the Ponomarev affair."

"And you're telling me all this in a hotel room?"

Richards cast his eyes around the room.

"We can talk here with safety. The hotel is clean."

"What is it you wish to know, sir?"

"I want to know exactly where you've gotten to and what you think at this stage of the game." Richards looked at his watch. "My plane leaves in an hour and a half. We have plenty of time."

Saunders gave Richards a blow-by-blow account of everything he had done between leaving Miami Beach and breaking into the Zentralstelle. The story of the incident at the archives and the unconscious guard gave him some trouble. He watched his boss closely to see how he took it. No reaction. The expression on his tight pale face remained sealed, as always. But what Richards didn't realise was that his mask provided the answer Saunders had been looking for.

When Jeff had finished his recital, Richards asked bluntly: "What are your conclusions?"

"Something happened in Block 13 at Dachau thirty years ago. I think those eight names with the red crosses, and the guard—Müller—were involved in it. Of those eight, two died during the past few years and two others—Slobodin and Dragunsky—have been murdered. That leaves four for whom we have addresses. These men must know the answer. Maybe one of them would be willing to talk. We should also try to get our hands on Jean-Marc Luçot and find out why he's so interested in these people. Is he operating under orders from the Editions Fontenoy, or is he on his own? And is he motivated solely by the manuscript *Letters in Blood*?

"I've come to Paris to find Luçot, see the manuscript, and meet the owner of Editions Fontenoy. At the same time, I'd like our agents to find the four remaining survivors and interrogate them. I would think that could be done in the next twenty-four hours."

Richards was silent for a moment, then nodded in assent. "That sounds logical to me. I can give you two or three more days. But no more. The Russians are really putting on the pressure. If we don't get to the bottom of this soon, things are going to go very sour in Moscow."

The C.I.A. chief put his glass down on the table. "Now, to practical matters: we have established a European headquarters for this operation in the embassy here in Paris. It's entirely at your disposal. We've put Jim Sullivan in charge." He gave a sly laugh. "For once, you'll have the rare pleasure of being his boss. He's selected some of the best men we have to work with you and to take on the less important assignments. They will handle all communications and telegrams. You're not to show your face anywhere near the embassy. They'll get in touch with you here about any operational details that come up."

He looked at his watch again. "Jeff, you've done a splendid piece of work. Keep it up."

He took his dispatch case, headed for the door, hesitated for a moment and turned around. "Jeff, I hope you don't mind that this conversation was taped for the Russians. It's the only way we can convince them of our good faith. You may even have to make a report to a group made up of both sides. Good God! Who ever would have thought that the C.I.A. would one day collaborate with the K.G.B. The day of judgment must be at hand!"

Jeff gave him a broad smile. "By the way, Hal, I was surprised there was no mention of the Zentralstelle incident in either press or radio."

Richards smiled back. "Rest assured, it won't be mentioned."

"That's exactly what I mean." Saunders suddenly turned

angry. "What do you think I am? Blind? An idiot? You send me off on a solitary mission and every place I go I'm followed by a train of baby-sitters to see that nothing happens to me. You think I didn't notice the car that shadowed me on the Autobahn to Ludwigsburg, or the guardian angel who knocked out the guard at the Zentralstelle? What are your men afraid of? That I'll fall on my face or trip an electronic eye for Christ's sake?"

Richards kept on smiling. "You're a bright fellow, Jeff. I always said you were. But you have to understand that this mission is of the greatest importance and I have to be absolutely sure that nothing happens to you. So we asked a few friends to follow you around and help you out if you needed it."

There was a discreet knock at the door.

"That's for me," Richards said. He held out his hand. "Goodbye, Jeff, and good luck."

"Hal!" Saunders jumped to his feet and stopped Richards before he could open the door. "Hal, we both remember the understanding we reached forty-eight hours ago, right? You asked me to take on a mission all by myself, and that's what you're going to get. So get those damned nursemaids off my tail and pronto! If you don't trust me, I take the first plane home. But if you want me to go on, I tell you here and now that if I ever find another bodyguard on my tail, I'll drop the whole shooting match and you and your Ponomarev can go to hell."

Richards smiled warmly. "As you wish, Jeff. From now on you work alone," and he turned on his heels and left.

"Monsieur ... ah ... Saunders—that is your name, is it not? No matter, no matter." Old Serge Fontenoy looked at his visitor with sly, intelligent eyes. Pointing a finger at him, he said: "You can say whatever you like, but I know the truth. You are an American agent!"

Saunders couldn't help laughing. The way Fontenoy had managed to unmask him was truly inspired. Sullivan's team had briefed him for over two hours on his "cover", preparing him down to the most minute detail. He had all kinds of letters of introduction; he had clothed himself in an identity that seemed absolutely watertight. And it hadn't taken the sharp old man two seconds to see through him.

Saunders decided it was best to say nothing.

The old man seemed to have read his thoughts. "All right. Don't say anything. After all, what else can you do? I've known you and your kind since before the war. You think you can fool everyone, don't you? What nonsense! I can smell an American agent at ten kilometres, I kept telling my old friends in the O.S.S. That surprises you? My dear young man, I was collaborating with the American secret service when you were still sucking on a bottle. Where do you come from? Minnesota? Idaho?"

Jeff smiled. "North Carolina."

"Of course, North Carolina. As I was saying, at that time, I was already working with your people. During the war, in the Maquis. Ask your elders: they'll tell you. Now that was work—real work. And there was only a handful of us. Of course, today every Frenchman claims he was with us. You ask anyone and he'll tell you he was in the Maquis, or at least some part of the Résistance. Scoundrels! Where were they when the Boches arrived? Hiding, like rats. Today they all sport the Legion d'Honneur and write epics about their exploits against the Germans. And who publishes them? I do! I publish their books and they sell like candy. But I assure you that when I was young, things were very different!"

"Sir, I ..." Saunders tried to stem the flow.

"So don't come telling me that you are here for an American publishing house and that you're a specialist in the history of Nazi atrocities. You're too young. You belong to another generation. The minute you started giving me that story about your so-called literary activities, I said to myself, either this boy takes me for a fool or he's an American agent!"

"Why does my age bother you?" Saunders asked. "After all, that boy who works for you—Luçot—is younger than I, and yet ..."

Fontenoy turned serious: "My dear friend, Jean-Marc Luçot lost his mother and father during the war. The Gestapo. He grew up in the shadow of those memories. He understands. I can guarantee that. In fact he understands too well.

104

Sometimes I worry that he is a prisoner of his memories, that he will never be able to free himself from them. That such a tragedy should be inflicted on a boy of such promise..."

The old man stopped, sunk in thought. Then he shook his head and his sharp little eyes began to sparkle again.

"How is it you speak such good French? A girl friend perhaps?"

You couldn't help liking the old man, Saunders thought. "No, my mother was French."

"Ah. Back to your business then. But first, take away all those papers." And Fontenoy shoved Saunders' letters of introduction towards him.

"I'm ready to help you. And you may tell your stupid bosses that they can come straight to Serge Fontenoy without all these childish stratagems that may fool your people but certainly not me. I will help you, but on one condition: you must give me your word that the information you want will not hurt my country. Can you swear to that?"

"Absolutely," Saunders said with relief. "I can guarantee more than that: my mission will actually help both our countries. I am also ready to..."

"Enough, enough," the old man said, holding up his hand. "I told you, your word is enough. So, what is it you want to know? What do you have against Jean-Marc Luçot?"

"Sir, you are even sharper than I had thought."

The old man gave a satisfied laugh. "Good. But I repeat, what do you have against him?"

"I'm not exactly sure that I have anything against him. He recently did some research and his results could be very useful to us. I would like to meet him, but I wanted to know first what you thought of him."

Fontenoy's eyebrows shot up. "You can't meet him here. He doesn't work for us any longer."

Saunders stiffened. "Why not? Did you fire him?"

"To tell you the truth, he never really worked for us fulltime. I knew his father before the war. An exceptional man. One of the great minds in French science. Had he lived, he would be one of our greatest physicists. He was involved in the attempt to transfer our heavy water out of France so that it wouldn't fall into German hands. The operation was a success, but Robert Luçot was arrested by the Gestapo. He was dragged from prison to prison and then we heard he had died. His wife was arrested too. A clever woman, but delicate. Those who knew her were afraid she would never survive prison life. She didn't. The boy, Jean-Marc, was brought up by relatives in complete poverty. Later, he went to the Sorbonne, fought in Algeria, was decorated several times. But in his private life, he was an unhappy man, haunted by morbid thoughts and the painful memory of his parents. He had trouble earning a living. He did some journalism, mostly for small left-wing papers. He tried to publish a novel, without success. I met him quite by chance and tried right away to help him. Even if I hadn't known his parents, I would have offered him a job here. He had an amazing fund of knowledge about the Nazi atrocities. I offered him a full-time job but he refused; he only wanted to work part-time as a reader. He was to advise us on the literary and documentary merits of all manuscripts having to do with deportations, the concentration camps, the 'final solution', that sort of thing. Recently we've seen less and less of him. I think he's involved with some girl. Somebody told me— I find it hard to believe—that he had been seen with a beautiful girl in some *boîte* on the Left Bank, and that they seemed crazy about each other.

"He left us ... let's see ... the beginning of June, I think. He didn't really leave us. He just came and said he would be away for several months. I made no objections. He'll undoubtedly come back and he'll be welcome. We've always been very happy with his work."

"Did he give you any reason for leaving?"

"No. But listen, I have his address. He might be home, but even if he isn't, he will have left a forwarding address."

"He had been working recently on a manuscript you plan to publish soon, isn't that right? It's called *Letters in Blood*, I think?"

Fontenoy looked at him with surprise. "Who told you we were going to publish that book?"

Saunders was caught short: "You're not going to?"

"I don't know yet. We haven't decided. The manuscript came ... when was it ...? I can find out right away." He pressed the button on his intercom: "Jacqueline, would you please bring me the file on *Letters in Blood*? You know, the Dachau manuscript. Thank you."

He turned to Saunders. "It was submitted to us and I remember giving it to Luçot to read. But so far as I know, he hasn't returned it yet. These things often take time, you know."

Saunders' thoughts were racing ahead. If this was true, then everything Luçot had told Schneider and the Zentralstelle about the book's imminent publication was pure invention. Was this possible?

There was a light knock on the door and a thin old lady walked in. "Monsieur Fontenoy, the manuscript isn't here. All I found in the file is this note." She handed Fontenoy a slip of paper which he read out loud: "Sent to Jean-Marc Luçot for reading on May 3rd. Sole copy."

"This is a fine state of affairs!" the old man exploded. "I remember that manuscript. It was the original, and there were no other copies. It was the journal of a Dachau prisoner who died during deportation. He had managed to hide the manuscript before his death. What made the manuscript unusual, horribly so, was that it was written with the author's own blood. Those brownish lines on the paper made me shudder."

"How did it happen to come to you?"

"Somebody found it while they were doing some construction work at Dachau and got in touch with a publishing house in Munich. Monument Verlag, I think. They didn't want to publish it for fear it would stir things up in Germany, so they sent it to me. They still hold the rights but we have an option. I must say that I think it's a little strange that he didn't return the manuscript. Luçot is such a dependable boy ... curious. But take his address and perhaps he will show it to you at his house." The old man scrawled a few words on a piece of paper.

Saunders suddenly had an idea: "Tell me, Monsieur Fontenoy, how long after you gave Luçot the manuscript did he announce he was leaving?"

Fontenoy thought for a moment. "I never put the two together. But wait a minute. I think it was the same day we signed the merger with Editions Chastet. I remember he talked to me between sessions in our negotiations. Just a moment . . ."

He reached for a leather-bound calendar on his desk and slowly turned the pages. Finally he looked up.

"We signed the contract on May 5th. So that's the day Luçot left."

Saunders jumped to his feet. "Two days after he received the manuscript!"

He shook Fontenoy's hand and without further ceremony, bolted from the room.

At four in the afternoon, four men walked casually—to all outward appearances—into the entrance of a large run-down house at 117 Rue de l'Ancienne Comédie, not far from the Boulevard Saint-Germain. Tom Butler, one of the task force at Saunders' disposal, led the others to the fifth floor. While they stood in a protective circle around him, Butler took out a bunch of keys and tried one after the other in the ancient lock.

"Don't be nervous," he whispered to Saunders. "He isn't home. As soon as you gave me the address, I came by and had a little chat with the concierge. I told her I was a foreign journalist who had known Luçot on *La Nouvelle Gauche*. She said that Luçot was doing a lot of travelling these days and was seldom home. According to her, he was here Monday and left the next day."

He kept trying the keys as he spoke. "Ah, there we are!"

The heavy door creaked open and the four men walked into the shuttered apartment. Tom Butler and the other two—Chuck Adams and a young Frenchman named Jean Laporte—fanned out on tiptoe.

Saunders walked through the shabby hall into a large room. He flipped the switch and suddenly the room was bathed in a harsh light.

Directly in front of him, between two crooked wall sconces, hung a .32 calibre Winchester Special.

8

"So you've found your murderer," Jim Sullivan said.

The C.I.A. chief of operations walked slowly into the room, took off his jacket and mopped his brow. "The French can build atomic submarines but they still haven't gotten around to air-conditioning." He lit a cigarette and cast a suspicious eye around the room.

It was seven o'clock. For three hours, the men had combed the apartment: closets, cabinets, the hundreds of books on the shelves, drawers, dispatch cases, every scrap of paper. Saunders had watched the procedure with admiration: first one man photographed every object, then another examined it for fingerprints and analysed them on the spot. They had decided to call Jim Sullivan at headquarters only towards the end of their search.

Sullivan stared at the rifle hanging on the wall.

"You really think he's the murderer?"

Jeff disregarded the question. "Come, I want to show you something."

He led Sullivan into Luçot's study, a small dusty room in wild disorder—dirty clothes, empty coffee cups, cigarette butts, books and papers scattered on the faded couch, on the wobbly desk, on what remained of a pale grey rug. Opposite the window stood a large armoire with glass doors.

"What do you make of that?" Saunders asked.

Sullivan let out an admiring whistle. "There's enough there to arm a battalion!"

It was only a slight exaggeration. The armoire, true to its original purpose, was packed with arms: revolvers, guns, knives. The revolvers were of various models: Walther P.P.K., Beretta, several Smith & Wessons, and a whole collection of French, Belgian, German and Japanese make. There were boxes of ammunition next to each gun. The rifles, standing in a neat row, were mostly recent models, most of them precision rifles. Two of them were American, there was a Belgian F.N. 37, and three with telescopic lenses made in Japan. There was also a hunting rifle and a semi-automatic R.S. of the type used in the French Army.

On top of the armoire were a half dozen silver cups. Sullivan read off the inscriptions, emphasising each word with his terrible French accent: *"Championnat de tir, Armée Française, Barbizon, 12-17 Juillet 1964—Premier Prix.* A champion, eh?"

Saunders elaborated: "Our client was the champion marksman in the French Army for four years, with both standard rifle and precision carbine. He won third place in the national championship for revolvers. He has a drawerful of medals and certificates showing that from 1960 to 1964 he had no equal. For some reason he stopped after that, but during the past six months he's been entering competitions again and won two more prizes."

"What condition are the guns in?" Sullivan asked.

"Ready to use. They're all in perfect condition—greased, adjusted, and with a sizeable reserve of ammunition."

"Everything legal?"

"Absolutely. He has a permit for every one of them. I suppose a marksman in his class would have no trouble getting permits."

"What about fingerprints?"

"On the guns, only his. In the apartment, we found two sets, his and somebody else's. It looks like he shared the apartment with a girl. Hair on the pillows, woman's clothing in the closet, cosmetics and . . . this."

Sullivan looked at the large photograph in a black leather frame on top of the bureau.

"Your friend has good taste."

The girl in the photograph was indeed disturbingly beautiful: a mass of blonde hair, a perfect face, a deep searching look in her eyes.

"The other fingerprints are hers?"

"It looks like it."

Sullivan returned to the living room, followed by Saunders. "Should we run a ballistics test on the Winchester?"

"Don't be an ass, Jim. That isn't the gun he used in the murder. He may have practised with it, but he certainly didn't use it to kill Ponomarev. He must have bought the murder weapon in New York, or Miami, or anywhere in the United States. You know perfectly well he would never have been allowed to board a plane for America with that gun. They've been making meticulous searches since all the hijackings started."

"So you're convinced he's the murderer?" Sullivan asked again.

"Yes, and I don't like it at all."

"Why? Why do you say that?"

"It's too simple. I start on a job that looks like it's going to be very complicated and suddenly the solution is dumped in my lap. I discover that all the victims knew each other at Dachau; I find Mr. Luçot's tracks all over the place; and in Mr. Luçot's own apartment, I discover the weapon, and proof that he's an outstanding marksman. Naturally, only an outstanding marksman could have brought off those murders. No, it's just too damn pat, too straightforward. All we need now is to find the motive for the murders which is undoubtedly hidden somewhere around here, trap our murderer and deliver him all done up and gift-wrapped to our pals in the Supreme Soviet. No, Jim, it smells funny."

"Maybe this is all some kind of put-on?" Sullivan said without conviction.

"No. The fingerprints are authentic, so are the permits. All these things can be verified; and that's exactly what I don't like about it. You look for a man who's been running around America killing people right and left and you find he's gone everywhere under his own name. You go to his house and you find an arsenal. No attempt to hide, or attempt to cover his tracks. As if he didn't give a damn if he was caught."

"Maybe he doesn't give a damn?"

Saunders shrugged.

Tom Butler came running into the room in a state of great excitement. He was carrying a package wrapped in old rags.

"We just found this in one of the closets between some empty shoe boxes and old blankets. I think it may be what you've been looking for."

Saunders took the package and placed it carefully on the table in the middle of the room. He undid the wrapping, exposing a sheaf of pages of different sizes. There were sheets of regular writing paper, pieces of dirty wrapping paper, others with German printing on the backs—slogans, S.S. propaganda, announcements.

On one side, the pages were covered with almost indecipherable writing. The lines were crooked, the letters misshapen. The five men stood around the table, their eyes fixed on the handwriting. It was a rusty brown colour.

"*Letters in Blood,*" Jeff Saunders said.

My name is Georges Brisseau. I was born in Grenoble, France. But my name and where I come from have lost all importance. They have been replaced by a number. Today, I am an anonymous number printed on a prison uniform next to a red triangle signifying that I am a "political prisoner". My number is K.Z. 762 983, Dachau. I am subhuman because I am a Communist. That is why I am condemned to death. When? I don't know. Perhaps as long as my physical strength holds out, I will be able to put off the day when I will be taken to the gas chambers and from there into the ovens. But it's only a matter of time. I lost hope long ago. I have known for a long time that I was only a living corpse. A dead man who can still walk, talk, think, feel, and even laugh sometimes. But all that's an illusion. Many of my comrades have already left this earth without resisting. My younger brother who worked with me in the Party in Grenoble threw himself against the electrified fence to put an end to his suffering.

When I was young, I dreamed of becoming a famous writer. Now I am thirty-five. I will never be a famous writer. I will never be anything but a small heap of ashes and charred bones that my companions in misery will remove from the ovens of Dachau. Maybe there will come a day when this camp is freed and its horrors exposed. But nobody will believe them. And one thing is certain: there will be no one here to describe how it was. We, this army of shadows dragging our feet down the valley of death, heads shaved, in striped uniforms and heavy wooden shoes, we won't be here. And maybe this place will never be freed. Germany is powerful and cruel. Perhaps she will rule the earth for centuries and centuries. Yet, if a better day should ever come, the world must know. It must know what happened here at Dachau, and in the other camps scattered across a Europe in chains.

That is why I have sworn I will write the truth about Dachau. I will describe everything I have seen, everything I have gone through and felt. I don't know if I will ever finish this book. I may be sent off to die tomorrow or the day after. But so long as I have an ounce of energy left, I will write. Perhaps by some miracle these pages will not be destroyed, and those who find them will learn that there is no limit to horror or degradation.

My closest friends have promised that if I die, they will bury this manuscript at Dachau. And if one of them should survive, he will return and unearth it. They have also promised to provide me with paper so that I have something to write on. I have a goose quill that I sharpened myself, but I have no ink. So I will have to write this book with my blood. Every day, I will cut myself and squeeze out a few drops of blood. With these drops I will write the truth about the blood that flowed at Dachau. May God help me.

Dachau, December 12th, 1943.

There was a stricken silence in the room. The men around the table stood as if paralysed by this cry of despair from another world. Thirty years after the faceless prisoner at Dachau had dipped his goose quill in his open wound, his words evoked in them a sharp, living pain. They had suddenly entered the world of the dead.

113

Saunders was the first to speak. He tried to sound matter-of-fact and efficient, but his voice was unsteady. "Let's divide up the work. We all know French. I'll separate the pages into five lots and each of us will read as fast as he can. What we're looking for is anything to do with Block 13 and specifically the names of Dragunsky and Slobodin." He pulled the list he had copied at the Zentralstelle from his pocket. "Here are some other names. Check this list as you read. I can feel it. What we're looking for is going to be in this manuscript."

The last page of the manuscript was numbered 196. Saunders divided up the pages and handed them to the men around the table. Then he lit a panatella and sank into the lopsided chair near the window. The first thing that impressed him was the author's obvious literary talent. He shuddered as he read the terrible tale. But there were no clues to the mystery in his pages.

A half hour had passed in complete silence when Jean Laporte cried out: "Jeff, I think I have it!"

They all ran to Laporte. "Look. Look at the bottom of the page dated December 23rd, 1944."

Jeff, who had squeezed in between Butler and Sullivan, focused on the last paragraph and read out:

Little by little, hunger and pain are erasing what little humanity we have left. We have gradually turned into a band of wild animals motivated only by the instinct for survival. God, what is happening to us? Tonight, a ghastly tragedy occurred in Block 13. Ghastly even by our standards, perverted by this hell of Dachau. I wasn't in the block when it happened, but I learned the whole story from the report Sturmführer Joakim Müller ordered me to take to the Camp Kommandantur. The Germans have decided to keep the thing secret and I am not going to speak of it either. It is too appalling. The state of famine in Block 13 . . .

"Where's the next page, Jean?" Saunders asked with impatience.

Laporte handed him another page. Saunders started reading again.

"...in the orchards of the region. Today again, another thirty political prisoners were sent to the gas chambers and..."

"This can't be it," Saunders said irritably. "Jean, I asked you for the page that follows the one I was reading. Where is it?" Saunders looked at the page in his hand. "We were on 92 and you've given me 95. Where are the two missing pages?"

Jean Laporte went through his lot again. "That's all I've got, Jeff. They're exactly in the order you gave me. Those two pages follow each other. It goes from page 92 to page 95."

In despair, Saunders let the sheets fall on the table. "He's had us again."

Pages 93 and 94 were missing from the manuscript.

Fifteen minutes later, there was a gentle knock on the door.

Silently the agents moved quickly and expertly into position. Butler and Adams pulled out their revolvers and flattened themselves on either side of the door. Jean Laporte dashed for the light switch. The apartment went completely dark and Jim Sullivan, with an agility unusual in a man of his girth, pulled Saunders after him into another room.

"There's nothing to worry about," he whispered. "It can't be the concierge. She got a telegram this afternoon saying her daughter in Arles was very sick and took the three fifty-five train. She won't be back until tomorrow morning. To anybody else, Luçot is not at home."

The knocking continued, this time in a definite cadence. Two long then three short knocks.

Laporte appeared at Sullivan's side. "It's O.K. It's one of our men."

"Open up then," Sullivan said sharply.

The front door was unlocked and a man slipped into the apartment.

"You can turn on the light," Tom Butler's voice said. "It's Bobby Marciano."

Sullivan went up to Marciano—a small, supple man with a shrewd face.

"I told you not to come here," Sullivan barked.

"It's very important, boss. I had to see you right away."

Marciano pulled an envelope from an inside pocket, took out three pieces of paper and placed them next to each other on the big table.

Jeff glanced at them over Sullivan's shoulder. The first was a newspaper clipping with a photograph and a brief story. It must have been in a prominent place on the first page because it showed a part of the paper's heading and date: *Le Courrier de Lyon* of June 14th. Saunders looked closer. The photograph showed a bald, smiling man with sharply etched features who looked around sixty-five. The caption under the picture read: "Mysterious murder of Michel Talbot." The story went on:

It was with concern and deep sorrow that we learned tonight of the sudden death of our aeronautical correspondent, Michel Talbot, who was killed by two shots from a revolver at the door to his home at 145 Avenue General de Gaulle in Villefranche. The police have no clues as to the identity of the murderer or the motive for the crime. The possibility of burglary has not been discounted. Last night, at about eleven thirty, Madame Talbot heard what sounded like explosions. Although she was already in bed, she quickly put on a dressing-gown and went out. The Talbot family lives in a small, isolated house in Villefranche. Madame Talbot found her husband lying on the sidewalk in front of the door. He had died instantly. He lay next to his blue Renault which was parked in front of the house; the engine was still warm. The keys to the car were in the dead man's hand.

Madame Talbot immediately alerted her neighbours and the police who arrived soon after. The coroner pronounced M. Talbot dead and the body was taken to the Hospital Antoine in Villefranche. Preliminary investigations reveal that Talbot was killed by two bullets from a Colt .45, both of which struck his head. The police found footprints behind a bush where the killer had apparently hidden while waiting for his victim. No empty cartridges were found. Thus it seems probable that the murder was committed by professionals. Madame Talbot told the police that she had heard no sound of a car driving off after the murder. However, a bicycle stolen earlier from a near-by house was found at some distance, at the intersection of Avenue General de Gaulle and Rue Lamartine. It is assumed that the murderer or murderers parked their car at this intersection and one of them rode the bicycle to the site of the murder. Once the crime was completed, the murderer bicycled back to the intersection, abandoned the vehicle and drove off in the waiting car.

Michel Talbot was born in Dijon in 1908, and had worked for *Le Courrier de Lyon* since after the Liberation. Before the war, he was a reporter on aeronautical subjects for *Le Temps* in Paris. During the war he organised and directed one of the most important cells of the Résistance, the "Renaissance", which operated in central France, committing acts of sabotage and relaying information to the Free French Forces in London. Arrested by the Gestapo, Michel Talbot was deported to Dachau on October 20th, 1943. In spite of the terrible conditions of his incarceration, he managed to survive until the Liberation and returned to France to resume his career as a journalist.

The sudden removal of this devoted colleague and faithful friend is a heavy loss to his friends and particularly to his fellow workers on *Le Courrier de Lyon*, and in the Association of Aeronautical Specialists of the French press whose president he had been for eight years. We extend our heart-felt sympathy to his widow, Madame Talbot.

Saunders and Sullivan looked at each other. "There's another one gone," Saunders said. "He was killed over two months ago: from the date, it looks like the first. He was shot only a few days after Luçot got the addresses from the Zentralstelle."

The second sheet was a copy of a telegram without any heading—no sender, no sendee—nothing that would make it possible to identify either in case it fell into the wrong hands. This was regular C.I.A. procedure for all telegrams sent from the U.S. Embassy. The telegram was brief:

Sent from: Capetown, 301430

Received by: Paris, 301857
Decoded by: b/287 542
For: Potomac/2
From: Pegasus
Marc Brajinski 72 Lord Kitchener Avenue Capetown murdered in his garage by revolver shots 3.8 Beretta June 28th at 00.30 Stop Two coloured suspects arrested after the crime released for lack of evidence Stop Investigation continues End

The third document was an ordinary piece of notepaper. Someone had written on it: 'Jean-Marc Luçot, French passport No. 233897, boarded plane for Israel Tuesday August 28th, Air France Flight 252 at four fifty p.m. with round-trip Paris Tel Aviv Paris ticket No. 55429786."

Saunders pulled the list of eight names from his pocket, took out his pen and made small crosses next to Michel Talbot and Marc Brajinski. There were only two names left, Johann Cyrankiewitz of Lodz, Poland, and Lev Jourbin of Israel.

"Did you make any enquiries in Poland and Israel?" Saunders asked Sullivan.

"Yes, but as you know, it's much tougher to get information out of those two countries. Poland is on the other side of the Iron Curtain and Israel is not very co-operative."

"Well, it doesn't make much difference. Maybe Luçot's been to Poland already; maybe he hasn't. The important thing is that our man left for Israel the day before yesterday. He's probably still there."

"What do you plan to do?"

"Take the first plane for Israel. Find out when the next plane leaves for Tel Aviv, will you? Then get me the most complete dossier possible on Jean-Marc Luçot. I want every detail from the day of his birth to today. There's only one place that will have that information and that's the D.S.T.* archives here in Paris. I've got to have it. I assume you have methods for handling special cases. And I trust you consider this a special case."

*Direction de la Surveillance du Territoire, the French equivalent of the F.B.I.

118

Tom Butler came over with an Air France schedule in his hand.

"There's a flight to Tel Aviv, leaving a quarter past midnight—an Air France Boeing 707. The next flight is tomorrow morning at seven fifty. An El Al Boeing, Flight 341 from New York."

"I'll take the one tonight if you can get me the dossier on time," Saunders said.

Sullivan looked at his watch. It was eight five p.m.

"You don't give me much leeway. I can't promise you anything. You know the café Le Paris on the Champs Elysées near the Franklin Roosevelt Métro station?"

"Yes."

"O.K. Go there and wait. One of us will meet you as soon as possible and tell you what we've found. We'll also take care of your ticket and the rest of the stuff."

"I'll be there."

"And don't worry about this apartment. We'll put everything back in place."

"In a few days, it won't make much difference."

He opened the door and disappeared down the dark stairs.

It was ten forty-five p.m. For over two hours, Saunders had given his undivided attention to the pin-ball machine manufactured by Gottlieb and Sons, of Chicago—an essential prop in every French café. His nerves were on edge; he jiggled the flashing machine and sent silver balls rolling towards the clowns and the bosomy girls scattered over the board. It just wasn't his lucky day. The scoreboard had yet to light up. He had just inserted another franc in the slot when he heard a voice behind him.

"May I?"

Saunders automatically stepped aside to let the Frenchman insert his money and join the game. The new player was Jean Laporte. He rested his cigarette on the edge of the machine, pulled the lever towards him and, brows knit with concentration, sent a ball flying. As he worked the flippers, his eyes fixed on the machine and, his voice almost drowned out by the constant tic-tac and ringing of bells, he said to Saunders:

119

"You have a reservation on both Air France Flight 272 tonight and El Al 341 tomorrow morning. You'll find your tickets at the Orly information desk to the right of the main entrance. All you have to do is show your papers, take your ticket and board the plane.

"Also, about the material you asked for. Our friends ... Damn! I blew it!" He said loudly: "Your turn, Monsieur."

Saunders muttered: "Go on, talk fast," as he sent a ball flying and began to torture the flippers.

"Yes, the material you asked for. Our friends—that is, our friends at the D.S.T.—can get at the dossier but they refuse outright to hand it over to us for even one minute. So we have arranged for one of their people to be on your plane. The agent will have the file with him. During the course of the flight, he will give you all the information they have on Luçot. He'll leave you at the Lod airport."

"They really have a dossier on Luçot then," Saunders said, giving Laporte a turn at the machine.

"Sure. Especially since the guy was an extreme leftist a while back."

"You're sure one of their men will be on the Air France plane tonight?"

"It depends." Laporte hunched over and shook the machine in a frenzy. "They don't want to send somebody for nothing. Their agent will board the plane only after they've made sure you picked up your ticket."

"How will I know him?"

"Don't worry about that. He'll know you."

"Did you get official approval from the D.S.T.?"

Laporte laughed. "Absolutely not. But we have our methods. Just a second..." He knocked the ball straight at the clown with the idiot face who spun into a wild dance. "I won!" Laporte shouted in triumph. "Thank you, Monsieur. Better luck next time."

Saunders put a ten-franc note on the counter, downed his drink, and left.

His rented Citroën D.S., elegant and ugly as a toad, was parked in the Rue Galilée. He set off down the half-empty streets towards the Autoroute du Sud. It was eleven fifteen. With luck he could make it. In twenty minutes he should be at the Orly Hilton where he had left his bags, then another ten minutes to the airport.

He floored the accelerator, caught the last light as it was turning yellow and entered the autoroute. He was certain he would get his hands on Luçot this time.

He was reaching to light a panatella when he noticed the white Aston-Martin. It passed him, swerved back into his lane with a squeal of tires and stopped abruptly. He knew what was coming—a thousand alarms went off in his head and his body stiffened for the coming impact. In a last desperate effort, he yanked the wheel to the right but the car went out of control and ripped into the guard rail. There was a terrible jolt and he lost consciousness.

He didn't want to wake up. He could feel gentle hands probing his body, his head, his arms, and a woman's warm voice was saying: "He's all right. Nothing is broken. Help me get him into my car." He felt himself being lifted by powerful arms onto the soft back seat of a car. A phrase kept repeating itself in his ear until it dawned on him that he was being asked a question. He had trouble moving his lips: "Orly Hilton ... Orly Hilton ..."

He felt the car stop and heard the girl saying: "Will you help me get him to his room ... No, it's nothing serious. He was in a car accident. It's just shock and a few bruises."

He was helped out of the car, through the lobby and into the elevator. The man kept asking questions and the girl repeated: "He'll be all right ... He'll be all right ..."

He was placed on a bed with the greatest care. The fairy-tale voice said: "Thank you so much. I can look after him now." And the male voice answered: "Don't hesitate to call if you need anything. Good night, mademoiselle."

He blacked out again and awoke what seemed like many hours later when he felt something cold on his forehead. He slowly opened his eyes.

He was on his bed at the Orly Hilton. The room was dark except for the moonlight which came in between the open curtains. The fresh air felt good and he realised that he was naked from the waist up. There was a small noise to his right and he turned his head.

The girl was sitting on the adjoining bed, leaning forward and holding a damp towel to his forehead. The moonlight shone on her blonde hair and outlined her slender figure against the open window. She saw that he was awake but didn't speak. Instead she stroked his face, his cheeks, his forehead. He let out a moan; she moved over to his bed.

Her voice was gentle. "Your face is bruised but it will be all right soon. You weren't seriously hurt."

With great difficulty, he managed: "Who are you?"

"I'm called Chris by my American friends."

"How do you know I'm American?" he said, raising himself on his elbows.

She laughed. "Don't forget I'm the one who brought you here and undressed you. I saw your papers. Your name is Jeff Saunders."

"Why did you bother to bring me here?"

There was a pause. "You won't believe me."

"Try it anyway."

She shook her long hair. "Some day perhaps ... Let's just say for now that I was concerned when I saw you unconscious in your car."

He felt his strength slowly coming back. He motioned towards the small bar near the window. "Will you have a drink with me?"

"Let me bring you something."

The whisky worked like a current through his veins. His brain began to clear and he suddenly sat up.

"Good God, what time is it? How long have I been here?"

She looked at her watch. "It's quarter past one."

He swore under his breath. She laughed again.

"You must be feeling better if you can swear like that."

"You were the one driving the Aston-Martin? Why..." He stopped abruptly.

She made a quick move to stand up. "I think it's time I left..." She started for the door, hesitated for a moment, and turned around.

"Are you really sure you're all right?" she said anxiously. "You don't need me any more?"

"Yes I do, Chris," Saunders said with a different note in his voice. There was a silence. She returned and sat on the edge of his bed, her hand resting on the bedclothes.

"What do you want?"

Almost boyish, he said: "I want you to stay."

She said nothing.

All of a sudden, it was wonderfully simple.

At six the next morning, he slid out of bed, dressed quickly, planted a kiss on the mane of blonde hair spread out over the pillow, gently touched the bare shoulder showing above the covers, and tiptoed towards the door. The delicious savour of the night was still with him; he could feel it all over his flesh. In the taxi on the way to the airport, Chris's face danced before his eyes, that perfect face he had seen for the first time in a black leather frame on Jean-Marc Luçot's bureau.

9

THE YOUNG WOMAN WHO TOOK THE SEAT NEXT TO HIM IN EL Al's first class was a big girl with blue eyes and long chestnut hair. But these advantages were cancelled out by a prim expression and dowdy clothes. When she put on her glasses and started scolding him like a school marm, his heart sank still further. On the other hand, it was something of a relief to be faced for once with a woman he didn't have to charm. So he gave her an innocent smile when she asked: "Where were you last night? I waited to the very last moment. Because of you I had to spend the night at the airport hotel."

"I'm so terribly sorry." And, pointing to his bruised and swollen face, he said: "I had an extraordinary night of love."

"Very amusing."

"I knew you wouldn't believe me," Saunders said and attacked his breakfast with gusto. He glanced around the compartment and noticed with relief that there were only two other passengers three rows ahead. "You work for the D.S.T. full-time?" he asked sceptically, half-way through his omelette.

"That is none of your business. You are only supposed to ask me questions about a certain man. I am to make this trip with you and give you specific information. That is all."

"But tell me," he said, still teasing, "won't it look a bit odd to have you go to Tel Aviv with me and then go back to Paris on the same plane. Or don't you think of things like that in your shop?"

She smiled for the first time and said with a hint of pride:

124

"Don't worry. Everything has been arranged. I am changing planes at Tel Aviv and going on to the Far East, stopping first in Teheran and Delhi. But in Teheran a telegram from my boss will be waiting for me, instructing me to return immediately to Paris. So, I'll be back in Paris by dawn tomorrow. It will be most difficult to find any connection between your flight and mine."

"O.K. then, let's get down to business. To whom have I the pleasure of speaking?"

"Mademoiselle Leroy," she said with emphasis on the "mademoiselle".

From a large flight bag at her feet she extracted two brown envelopes marked I and II in black Indian ink. She took a set of papers out of the first envelope. They were photocopies of the original documents. Obviously Sullivan's friends at the D.S.T. were prudent men. Once their conversation was finished, Mademoiselle Leroy would destroy the copies and no one would be able to prove that any documents concerning J.-M. Luçot had ever left the D.S.T. archives.

She began reading from the papers in her hand:

"Jean-Marc Luçot: born in Paris, May 11th, 1940. His father, Robert Luçot, was a physicist. His mother, Anne-Marie, maiden name Montsel, was originally from Nancy. The father was arrested by the Gestapo in August 1940. He was first incarcerated in a series of French prisons, then deported to Germany where he was interned successively at Buchenwald, Neuengamme and Mauthausen. At this point, all trace of him was lost. After the war, the Red Cross indicated that he had died during deportation, but it is not known whether it was at Mauthausen or some other camp. The mother, Anne-Marie, died during interrogation on February 15th, 1942. She was tortured in the basement of the Sûreté in Paris where the Gestapo had established its headquarters.

"Jean-Marc was taken in by his mother's brother, Charles Montsel, the father of a large family. From earliest childhood, Luçot showed signs of anxiety, apparently due to the lack of maternal love. He had nightmares. He fought with the other children, locked himself in and kept to

125

himself. Twice he tried to run away. When he was old enough to enter the lycée, his uncle told him what had actually happened to his parents. The boy suffered a terrible shock and disappeared for several weeks. The police found him in the forest near Mont Valérien where there is a memorial to the men killed fighting the Nazis. The doctors examined him, found him in good physical condition but recommended psychiatric help. However, the Montsel family lacked the means to pay for treatment.

"Nevertheless, Jean-Marc grappled with his problems and matured early. He won a scholarship to the Sorbonne where he took courses in history, philosophy and French civilisation. It was during this period that he developed leftist tendencies and joined the Communist Party. He was active in Party affairs but his prime interest was in anti-German activities. He was arrested several times: in June '58, February and April '59, and January, March, April and September '60 and accused of organising student demonstrations against West Germany, and against Chancellor Adenauer's visits to France. He became an authority on the history of Nazism and Hitler's policy of genocide, organising meetings and seminars for Party members. He headed a delegation that visited the extermination camps in Germany and Poland. On his return he suffered a nervous breakdown and spent three months taking a sleep cure in a clinic in the Loire region.

"I have here the medical report made on his release from the clinic. Doctor Sauvage, the doctor in charge, indicated that Luçot was unstable and that although he might appear normal at times, he would be likely to suffer bouts of depression and paranoia, or even harbour ideas that might lead to violence.

"In 1960, he was drafted. I have a letter he wrote to a girl he was in love with at the time—Sylvie Duroc—in which he threatened to commit suicide. Among other things, he wrote: 'The ghosts of my mother and father haunt me day and night. I cannot rid my mind of their memory and I cannot go on living with the constant thought of their terrible fate.' We do not know if he actually tried to commit suicide at this time but another letter

126

tells us that he decided to join the Foreign Legion where, by exposing himself to all sorts of dangers, he would arrive at the same results.

"He was sent to Algeria and distinguished himself for bravery. All his superior officers praised him highly. Major de Valéry wrote on January 18th, 1961: 'Luçot is a disciplined soldier, although unsociable. In a combat situation, his courage is unmatched. He inspires this spirit of heroism in his comrades. He is also the best marksman in the Legion's 1st Regiment of Parachutists.' In point of fact, Luçot won all the championships in the French Army from 1960 to 1964. He was sent to officers' school in 1961 and when he returned to Algeria, he continued to show great courage. According to some sources, he showed unusual cruelty towards Algerian civilians. Later, his psychiatrists saw this as further proof of his instability and as a form of schizophrenia: he was half the Communist haunted by the memory of the Nazi atrocities, and half a merciless and cruel officer in the Foreign Legion.

"At the end of 1964—after a brief period as a career officer—he was demobilised and returned to France. Then followed a series of setbacks and personal crises. He tried to write, submitting articles to various leftist journals, but few were published. He wrote a bad novel about the death camps and it was rejected everywhere. For a time, he earned his living tutoring at a lycée. At the end of '66, he attempted suicide by slashing his wrists. He barely survived. In '67 he again spent several months in a psychiatric hospital. In '68 he left the Communist Party after the Soviet invasion of Czechoslovakia but was arrested and jailed in Paris for his participation in the demonstrations of May '68 and '69. In '71 he tried suicide again, this time with sleeping pills, but the dose was too small. Since '67, he has been employed part-time by Editions Fontenoy as a specialist on Nazi Germany, and on the extermination of Communists, Résistance fighters and Jews. In this capacity, he made several trips to Germany and Austria.

"Meanwhile, two of his father's brothers who had lived in Nice died and left him a little money—just enough to live on. He published several articles in the *Nouvel Ob-*

servateur and was on the fringes of Jean-Paul Sartre's circle. He helped make a film for French television marking the tenth anniversary of the capture of Adolf Eichmann.

"Throughout this period, he was almost always alone, with virtually no friends. He was never seen with girls. Then suddenly, in March of this year, he began to be seen with a beautiful girl named Christine de La Maleyne."

"Chris to her American friends," Jeff murmured.
"What did you say?" Mademoiselle Leroy asked sharply.
"Nothing. Nothing at all. Please go on."

"Christine de La Maleyne belongs to a family of the old nobility which owns the famous Château de Belvoir on the Loire. The family still lives in a wing of the château. She has a degree in literature and philosophy from the Sorbonne and has travelled extensively in Germany, the United States and the Far East.

"We do not know how they met, but we do know that starting in March, Christine and Jean-Marc were inseparable. They went everywhere together and, according to Luçot's concierge, she often spent the night with him. This affair caused considerable surprise. Christine is a beautiful girl from the best society, and was always surrounded by a flock of rich and handsome young men. Then suddenly she became attached to a man who at best cut a rather pitiful figure."

"The heart has its reasons..." Jeff said under his breath.
Mademoiselle Leroy gave him another disapproving look. "From May on, Luçot did a great deal of travelling. Are you interested in where and when he went?"
Saunders nodded.
"From May 5th to 10th—Vienna—round trip Air France. May 12th—to Stuttgart and back the next day, via Lufthansa. Another trip to Stuttgart, June 6th and 7th. June 15th—to South Africa via South African Airways—returned June 29th. July 22nd—trip to Canada and the United States via T.W.A. Returned to France August 26th. August 29th—to Israel via Air France. Round trip ticket."

The dates corresponded exactly with the murders.

Saunders asked: "Did Christine de La Maleyne ever go with him?"

Mademoiselle Leroy consulted the documents in the second envelope. "We don't know. If she did, we would have it here. Since it isn't, we have to assume he travelled alone. Or at least, he was alone on the plane trips. Obviously, they could have travelled separately and met abroad. Wait a minute ... maybe this will help. The concierge told us that Christine had a key to the apartment and that she sometimes used it when Luçot was away from Paris. But during the period he was in America and South Africa, she didn't go to the apartment once. I don't know how significant that is."

She continued leafing through the documents. "These are psychiatric reports, reports on his movements, copies of driver's licences, identification cards, passports, the concierge's reports, permits for possession of firearms, copies of articles he wrote ... Do you want to see these?"

"Please." Saunders carefully examined the documents as she handed them to him. Most of the firearms had been bought during May and June, just before the first murder.

"Do you have a photograph of him?"

She gave him two. The first showed a young man with piercing black eyes, wide forehead, dishevelled hair, thin nervous lips, and a slightly receding chin. Even in black and white, his pallor was noticeable. It was a young, rather agreeable face but the eyes stared out with a fierce intensity.

The second picture appeared to have been taken recently, without the subjects' knowledge. It showed Jean-Marc and Christine coming out of a house. Luçot, looking thin and worn, had his arm around Christine's waist. She looked taller than he, though it might have been an optical illusion. He was wearing a raincoat over a turtleneck shirt and had grown a scraggy beard—probably to hide his weak chin. Everything about him gave an impression of pain and tragedy.

The noise of shuffling papers reminded him of Mademoiselle Leroy's presence.

"Here is something that might interest you," and she handed him a photocopy of a receipt from the Villiers branch of the Crédit Lyonnais in Paris. It showed that the sum of a hundred thousand francs had been deposited in Jean-Marc's account (No. K/459768) on May 20th.

"That's almost twenty thousand dollars," Saunders observed.

"It was a cash deposit," Mademoiselle Leroy added.

The International Airport of the Promised Land greeted them with a blast of torrid air that seemed to come straight from Gehenna. Saunders immediately removed his jacket but his sweat-soaked shirt was no better. He watched with a certain amount of envy as the difficult Mademoiselle Leroy marched off towards the air-conditioned transit lounge. They were ready for him at the information booth. In the familiar monotone of her profession, an earnest hostess said: "Welcome to Israel, Mr. Saunders. Following instructions from American Express in Paris, we have made a reservation for you at the Tel Aviv Hilton. An air-conditioned Hertz Mustang is waiting for you in the parking lot, licence No. 283-786. Will you please sign here, and here. Thank you." She handed him a stack of tourist brochures showing happy Americans garlanded with cameras, fat cigars in their mouths, slapping kibbutz pioneers on the back, the Israelis wearing shorts and the national cap called the Tembel—meaning "idiot" in Hebrew, because of the fatuous look it gave the wearer. "Ordinarily you would have to confirm your return trip seventy-two hours in advance, but thanks to special arrangements between American Express and El Al, you need warn us only three hours before flight time. Hopefully, the plane will not be full. We trust you enjoy your stay in Israel, Mr. Saunders. Shalom."

He returned her tight smile, picked up his suitcase and headed into the noonday sun.

He found his silvery-green Mustang in the section of the parking lot reserved for rental cars. On the front seat was a road map of Israel which he examined with care. Since this was his first time in the country, he had automatically assumed that Ashkelon, where Jourbin lived, would be a considerable distance from Tel Aviv. He was delighted to find that the old Philistine city which the Jewish immigrants had rebuilt was actually only about forty miles from the airport. Instead of wasting precious minutes going to the hotel, he could just as well go directly from Lod to Ashkelon and make up some of the time so beautifully lost with Christine. He turned the air-conditioning on full blast, released the hand brake and set off with his usual squeal of tires.

The road shimmered in the heat and a thick haze hovered above the scorched fields. He made a right turn, passed the majestic ruins of the old part of town and found himself in the new city. It was two in the afternoon. The streets were almost deserted; the entire population seemed to be behind the lowered blinds of the vast white apartment houses, except for a few sitting in the cafés in the shade of gay parasols that lined the wide sidewalks.

He had little trouble finding Bialik Street, a quiet little road bordered by large trees that dropped towards the sea. In the distance, he could see the gold sand and the white crests of the waves breaking lazily against the shore. Number 18 was a small white cottage gleaming in the sun with a well-tended lawn in front. Saunders parked the Mustang next to the sidewalk and walked up a winding path laid in a mosaic of reddish stones.

He was about to ring the door bell when he noticed that the door was ajar. He knocked twice and when there was no answer, he pushed the door open and walked in.

There was no front hall: he found himself immediately in the large living room, and what he saw left him stunned. The room was packed. Most of the people were dressed in black. Three women, one young, the other two quite old, were sitting on the couch opposite the front door. An old man was trying to comfort one of the old women, holding her hand and patting her shoulder.

A very young officer in an open-necked khaki shirt was crouched on a low stool, a little apart from the others. A group of older men and women sat in a semi-circle and talked among themselves in low voices. They stopped when Saunders appeared at the door.

In a corner of the room, Saunders noticed a solitary candle burning on a small table. All the mirrors and pictures on the walls were draped in black.

The young officer got up and walked silently over to Saunders. "Shalom," he said softly.

"Do you speak English?" Saunders asked in a low voice.

"Yes."

"My name is Jeff Saunders. I've come from Paris to speak with Lev Jourbin."

The officer lowered his eyes. "I am his son. I am sorry, Mr. Saunders, but you have come too late. Lev Jourbin died the day before yesterday. We are sitting the seven days of mourning."

Once again, Saunders felt the humiliation of defeat. He asked the young man: "Could you go outside with me for a moment?"

The officer followed him into the sweltering street. But Saunders was beyond feeling the heat. He walked straight towards the sea and the young Israeli fell into step.

"I had thought ... I had hoped I could save your father's life. But I came too late."

Young Jourbin looked bewildered. "Save his life?"

It was Saunders' turn to be confused. He wanted to ask if the murderer had been caught but he decided to avoid direct questions. "How ... how did your father die?"

They had come to the end of the street and stood facing the sea.

The officer pointed directly ahead. "There, straight ahead of us ... He drowned there, the day before yesterday as he was taking his afternoon swim. As you see, the beach is completely deserted at this hour. We kept telling him that he swam too far out, that he wasn't careful enough. He was an old man, well past sixty."

Saunders tried to hide his amazement. "He ... he was here alone?"

"Yes, no one was with him. And he didn't really go out very far. He drowned right here near the beach. His body was found in less than an hour."

Saunders suddenly had the feeling that the thread he had been following so long and so hard was about to escape him.

"Did your father happen to see a young Frenchman who was here a few days ago?"

"You mean Luçot? Jean-Marc Luçot? Of course he was

here. He came by the night before my father died. He was still here the next morning, but he had to cut his trip short and return to Paris. My father drove him to his plane in the late morning. My mother said my father seemed very tired and depressed when he returned from the airport but he absolutely refused to skip his afternoon swim. That's what killed him." Young Jourbin was silent for a moment then looked at Saunders. "But how do you know about Luçot? And who are you, if I may ask?"

Saunders decided this wasn't the moment to be evasive. "I am an agent for Interpol. I came to Israel because we had information that a Frenchman named Jean-Marc Luçot intended to murder your father."

The young Israeli's eyes opened wide with astonishment. "Jean-Marc, murder my father? I never heard anything so absurd. Why would Jean-Marc murder his benefactor, his best friend?"

"They were friends?" Saunders' entire hypothesis seemed to be cracking up.

"Of course they were friends! My father did everything he could for Luçot, almost from his childhood. He sent him money, presents. He did everything possible to see that Jean-Marc lacked nothing. He even made two trips to France just to see him. They wrote each other about once a month. They were very close; he was like an adopted son to my father. I didn't know him because he had never come to Israel. I met him for the first time this week, but barely saw him. He spent most of the time closeted with my father. They had so much to talk about. My father cried like a child while Jean-Marc was talking to him, and as I told you, Mother said he was terribly upset when he returned from the airport. And after all that, you tell me he wanted to kill my father? It's ridiculous!"

Saunders looked at the young Israeli, bewildered. "Why were your father and Luçot so close?"

A shadow fell over the young man's face, as if he were dredging up a painful memory.

"My father was in the Red Army and was taken prisoner by the Germans. He was deported to a concentration camp where he made friends with Jean-Marc's father, Robert Luçot.

They were close to the very end. By some miracle, my father survived. Robert Luçot died. Literally in my father's arms. In Block 13 at Dachau."

Jim Sullivan was waiting for him at Orly. Saunders was on the point of alluding to the lapse in security, but didn't. This was no time for jokes. His sense of confusion had grown to desperate proportions while his plane neared Paris.

"Jim, I'm at a complete loss."

Sullivan said nothing. He waited for Saunders to continue.

"Everything's mixed up. I leave for Israel on Luçot's heels. As I drive to the airport, his girl friend contrives an accident that makes me miss my flight. I can't figure out how she knew who I was or how she found out I was on the tail of her Romeo. In any event, the incident proved to me that I was on the right track, that I almost had my hands on Luçot, that perhaps I still wasn't too late. And when I arrive in Israel, what do I learn? That Luçot had left forty-eight hours before, while I was still in Paris, meaning that Chris's maneuver was totally superfluous. On top of that, not only did he not kill Jourbin but Jourbin loved him like a son. I checked it all out: Luçot left Israel before Jourbin drowned; he did not stay behind without Jourbin's knowledge in order to murder him and make it look like an accidental drowning. Then, by God, I learn that Luçot's father was also in Block 13 in Dachau.

"What in Christ's name does it all mean? All this time, he has been calmly carrying out his little vendetta, killing them off one after the other, and suddenly it's over. Not to mention the fact that he had disappeared. Vaporised. Where the hell is Luçot, Jim? I cabled you from Tel Aviv. Did he return to France?"

Sullivan shook his head. "We're in a fog too. We know he took the plane at Tel Aviv. The plane stopped at Vienna, Munich and Geneva. He must have gotten off at one of those stops because he sure as hell hasn't come back here."

"He could have crossed the border by train or car."

"That's entirely possible." Sullivan made a gesture of helplessness. "The passport checks are very sketchy on trains and roads."

Saunders led Sullivan into a small bar in the airport basement and emptied two glasses of whisky in quick succession. He sat for a long time with his head in his hands.

"What do you plan to do now?" Sullivan asked almost timidly.

"There's only one thing left to do. The eighth man on the list, the Pole in Lodz. There's a plane for Warsaw in an hour and a half. I'm going to make it. The Pole is my last hope. Luçot *must* be there. There's no one else left on the list."

"Maybe he got off at Vienna and took a plane to Warsaw?"

"That's possible." There was a pause, then Saunders abruptly hit the chair with his fist. "Good God, Jim, here I thought I had the thing sewed up and it's all come apart."

"Come on. Don't be discouraged." Jim gave him an encouraging smile. "Go to Warsaw and we'll keep our eyes open here. I know you're going to make it."

"Knock it off, Jim. I'm not a twelve-year-old."

Sullivan accompanied him to the bus for Le Bourget. Saunders stopped at the LOT counter and bought a round-trip ticket for the eleven p.m. plane to Warsaw. He passed through customs once again and took a seat in the waiting room next to a group of Polish engineers, waiting for his flight to be announced.

But he did not take the plane to Warsaw that night.

"Monsieur Saunders! Monsieur Jeff Saunders! Please go to the information desk. You have an urgent call. Thank you. Monsieur Jeff Saunders, please go to the information desk. Thank you."

At first he couldn't believe it: his name broadcast over loudspeakers in an airport! They've gone mad! he told himself. Just forty-eight hours ago they were giving me all that crap about security measures and Paris being full of Chinese ... Either the Paris bureau of the C.I.A. has lost its mind, or something so important has happened that they have to get me and damn the precautions.

He walked over to the information desk. "I am Jeff Saunders."

"Monsieur Saunders, there is an urgent call for you, there in the corner—booth number 1."

He went into the booth and picked up the receiver.

"Jeff."

He knew the voice right away. There was a long pause. "Yes, Chris."

Her voice sounded weary, dead. The melodious tone that had charmed him when he first met her was gone.

"Jeff, don't go to Poland."

He was silent, paralysed.

"I've been trying to find you since early morning. I called every airline. I wanted to warn you. Cyrankiewitz isn't in Poland. He is here, in Paris. He emigrated illegally in 1948."

"Why are you telling me this?"

Her voice sounded more and more desperate. "I want to prevent another murder. It's time to stop this insane massacre."

He wanted to get back at her: "Why don't you tell Luçot yourself instead of ambushing and sleeping with his enemies."

"I never want to see him again. You can tell him that for me."

"Don't you love him?"

"No."

"Then for the love of God," he yelled into the receiver, "what is all this about?"

"I hope you never know," the toneless voice answered. "Do you have something to write with?"

"Yes."

"Take this down: Johann Cyrankiewitz lives alone at 75 Rue Chautemps in Montmartre. It's a two-story private house. There are no other tenants."

"So?"

"Jean-Marc intends to kill him tonight. If you hurry, you may be able to stop him."

"O.K."

"Jeff."

"Yes?"

"Be careful, I beg you. He's armed."

Saunders hung up.

*　　*　　*

136

The taxi left him at the street corner, about a hundred yards from Number 75. He looked at his watch. The driver had done well: twenty minutes from Le Bourget to Montmartre. A real achievement.

He walked slowly, hugging the walls, until he reached Number 75. It was a high, narrow house of grey stone, reminding him of the narrow old houses of Amsterdam. He gave a last look behind him. The street was dark and deserted. A dim light shone from the windows of the second floor.

He forced the lock on the door with his burglar's tools and found himself in a dark hall. Inching forward, he almost collided with an old bureau against the right-hand wall. He kept advancing until his hand touched the railing of the stairway. He tiptoed up the stairs, praying that the old dried wood wouldn't creak under his weight. On the second floor, he found himself in a dark hall. With infinite caution, he felt along the wall until he came to a door and slowly turned the knob. He held his breath and opened the door. He was in a large empty bedroom; the bed was unmade. He returned to the hall, closing the door behind him.

Silently, he moved over to the next door. It was not completely closed and a small ray of light showed through the opening. Again he held his breath and slowly pushed. The door swung noiselessly on its hinges and he took in the scene.

He was in a large studio. Around the walls were rows of antique armoires with glass doors. They were filled with hundreds of small stuffed animals—birds, lizards, squirrels, small wild animals. There were bookshelves to the ceiling, and mounted above the imposing marble mantelpiece, a large stuffed lion's head flanked by two antique Spanish lances. Blood-red velvet draperies hung at the windows.

The far end of the room was in darkness. The only light came from a small brass lamp standing on a large Louis XVI mahogany secretaire. The writing surface was padded with embossed black leather nailed to the wood with gleaming brass tacks. Against the secretaire and next to an ashtray in the shape of a death's head rested the top half of a man's body. All that was visible were two long white hands and a pale emaciated face with a wide forehead. In the middle of the forehead was a small hole oozing a trickle of blood which had dried on the black leather next to the little lamp.

The man had apparently been shot as he sat at his desk. He had probably jerked upright when the bullet hit, killing him instantly, then slumped forward on the table. He was wearing a black silk kimono.

As Saunders took a couple of steps into the room, he heard a small noise and felt a movement behind him. But he was too slow. Something hard hit the nape of his neck and a blinding flash exploded before his eyes.

He woke up to the sound of distant church bells ringing midnight. He was sitting in a high-backed old Spanish chair, bound to it by a fine nylon cord that bit into his flesh. He tried to move but he couldn't.

A faint noise caught his ear, and out of the corner of his eye he tried to see where the sound was coming from. Facing him, the dead man lay slumped on the secretaire as before.

A shadow glided forward from behind him. He waited on edge as a thin, stoop-shouldered figure moved past him and up to the secretaire. Then it turned around and he was face to face with Jean-Marc Luçot. Luçot was dressed in black from head to toe; his hair was dishevelled, his face pale, unshaven, his eyes almost dead. He held a Luger loosely in his hand and seemed almost unaware of the body sprawled near him.

"You know who I am." The voice was almost inaudible. "And I know who you are."

Saunders didn't speak.

"I didn't gag you because I didn't think you'd call for help. But even if you did, it wouldn't change anything. It's too late now."

Saunders licked his cracked lips.

"Why?"

"He was the last one. I've eliminated them all. Dragunsky, Slobodin, Talbot, Brajinski . . . all of them."

Saunders was silent.

"He was the last one," Luçot repeated. For a second, a look of triumph gleamed in his eyes. "It's time to lower the curtain. The hunt is over. I have my revenge. It's my turn to go now. Maybe I can finally rest. And my father too. They were with him at Dachau. You know about it, don't you. They were together in Block 13. Just one night. They got what they deserved. I killed them all."

"But why?" Saunders' voice was very low.

Luçot fixed him with his lifeless eyes. Then he crossed his hands over his chest and spoke very slowly.

"They killed my father. They tore him to pieces and ate his flesh."

There was a long silence before Saunders spoke.

"I don't believe it..."

Luçot did not speak. Supple and silent as a ghost, he disappeared from Saunders' field of vision. He was back a few seconds later and, without a word, placed two sheets of paper side by side on Saunders' lap. Even before Jeff's eyes took in the rust-coloured writing, he knew that Luçot had presented him with the key: the missing pages from *Letters in Blood*.

Luçot vanished again. Here, in this room, roped to a chair, alone with a dead Pole, spied on by the dead eyes of a hundred stuffed animals, he was about to learn the true background to Luçot's vendetta that had endangered the world.

...the hunger rampant in Block 13 has already broken the prisoners' spirit; they are close to madness. Most of them are Russian and Polish soldiers, but they have thrown in a few French, Belgians and Dutch. For six months, Block 13 has been a hell, a colony of the damned, forgotten by God and man. The Nazis have been starving them systematically. At the beginning, they just reduced their rations; then they fed them once a day, then once every other day, now once a week. No one knows whether the camp commander has ordered this or whether Sturmführer Joakim Müller is acting on his own initiative.

When the authorities set about starving the Russians and Poles, they knew the prisoners would end by killing each other over a piece of bread or a spoonful of soup. And that is what happened—while they still had the strength to fight. There was not only the blind hatred between Russians and Poles, but also the instinct for survival. How many were beaten up or trampled to death on their way to the soup kettles? How many were strangled under cover of night for a slice of bread? But it didn't last long. Little by little, the prisoners lost the energy to fight. They lay prostrate on their cots, and died one by one. During the last weeks in Block 13, the death rate reached a dozen a day.

By this week, there were only fifteen prisoners still alive. Most were dying, some were half-crazed. Then last night, two new prisoners were brought in: a Russian officer, Lev Jourbin, and a Frenchman, Robert Luçot. Luçot was tall and strong, in the prime of life. But he had been seriously injured that afternoon when a huge block of stone fell on him in the quarry where he worked. His friend Jourbin carried him on his back the eight kilometres back to camp. For some reason the Nazis did not kill him even though he was now useless to them. They just threw him and his friend into Block 13.

The fifteen prisoners left in the block were: Ivan Arnalski, Blagomir Pohatz, Michel Talbot, Marc Brajinski, Ladislas Stolkin, Tikhomir Boyartchev, Johann Cyrankiewitz, Arkadi Razumov, Arkadi Slobodin, Robert Mischo, Hendrik Van Velden, Anton Prihacz, a young man named Mishka who had gone mad long before—no one knew his family name, Stepan Dragunsky, and Yanek Spikhalski.

When I started this journal, I swore I would describe faithfully everything I saw and heard at Dachau. But I do not have the strength or courage to describe all that happened that night in Block 13. So I'll be brief: the prisoners in the neighbouring blocks say they heard horrible screams coming from Block 13. I learned what caused those screams from Müller's report. In the dark, the fifteen human skeletons left their cots and dragged themselves to where the wounded man lay. Crazed with hunger, they threw themselves on the helpless man, tore him to pieces and ate his flesh. A man like them, a man made in their own image. Dear God!

Saunders closed his eyes. He was trembling uncontrollably. The two sheets of paper slipped from his lap.

140

"Now you know the truth." Jean-Marc was back in the room.

He leaned over, carefully picked up the two sheets and placed them on the secretaire. Then he looked at Saunders. "I'm sure there are many more things you would like to know. I will tell you everything because you are the only one who will leave this place alive. For me, it's finished. This is where I end everything."

Saunders waited.

"For years I've been haunted by questions about my parents: How did they disappear? How did they die? What were their last moments like? I had little trouble finding out about my mother, but I could get no information about my father. All I knew was that Lev Jourbin who emigrated to Israel had remained his closest friend to the very end. But he never spoke to me about my father's death. I had nightmares; I saw him die a thousand times. Maybe my instinct told me that my father's death was ghastly even by the terrible standards of the concentration camps. But I knew nothing really."

"Until Fontenoy gave you the manuscript?"

"Yes, until Fontenoy gave me the manuscript. When I read it, I thought I would lose my mind. My first reaction was to commit suicide, to escape this insane world. I left Editions Fontenoy. I don't really know what I did for the next week. All I know is that it wasn't cowardice that kept me from putting a bullet through my head. I would have committed suicide if it wasn't for ... if it wasn't for ..."

"Christine?"

"Yes. Christine. She gave me the courage to go on. She helped me over the crisis. She understood. She supported me when I told her what I intended to do—that I was going to find my father's murderers and kill them one by one until they were all gone."

"How did you meet her?"

"I met her one night after one of my lectures on the Résistance. It was about six months ago. She came to see me and said that her father, Pierre de La Maleyne, had been in a Résistance group that operated in the Loire region. He had been caught by the Nazis and shot two months before she was born. She wanted to find out all she could about this period. We began to meet fairly often. I have to confess that at the beginning I wondered what a girl like her could see in me. But it went on and we ended up living together."

"Did she help you?"

"She was devoted to me. She did many things: she gave me courage when I was in despair; she sold a big property she had inherited from her father to help finance the operation; she went to the Zentralstelle to get additional information. Every time I did anything, she was at my side. Without her, I couldn't have done anything.

"Once I'd made up my mind, I went to see Schneider in Vienna, then found further information at the Zentralstelle. Christine was with me when I killed the first one—Michel Talbot. Call me sadistic if you like, but when I saw him die there on the sidewalk, I felt a savage satisfaction for the first time in my life. And I continued my revenge. I went to South Africa and killed Brajinski. It was child's play. Then we left for the United States."

"How did you get Slobodin's address?"

"Through Christine. She went to Ludwigsburg. By that time, the Zentralstelle had got his address through the help of a group of East European refugees. We went first to New York where we followed Slobodin and then to Miami to track down Dragunsky-Dragner. Nothing easier. It's very easy to commit a murder when you appear to have no motive. Once we had finished shadowing them, we returned to Montreal where we set the plan in motion."

"I know," Saunders said. "The telephone calls and reservations for the rooms at the Dauphine in Miami Beach."

"That's right—reservations, buying the weapons. We had no trouble whatever killing Dragner. No one suspected us. We weren't staying at the Dauphine and fifteen minutes after the murder, we were on our way back to New York. We mailed the gun air express."

"You took no precautions at all?" Saunders asked. "You literally left elephant tracks wherever you went?"

Luçot looked at him with his feverish eyes. "I didn't want to take precautions. At the start, I was careful only because I didn't want to get caught before I'd brought off my plan.

142

But I had no desire to hide my identity, cover my traces or fake what I was doing so that I could live to a ripe old age. On the contrary, I wanted the whole world to know. I wanted the world to know that Jean-Marc Luçot had avenged his father's death. The only thing that mattered to me was time. Time and efficiency. To make no mistakes and bring off my project."

"Yet you did make a mistake: Ponomarev."

"Yes. That was a serious mistake. We were after Slobodin ... and I shot Ponomarev. But how was I to know? That night in New York, I watched Slobodin go into the Plaza from a distance. Then I saw him come out a few minutes later and leave in his car. We followed him. On his way back to New York, Christine gave me the signal and I pulled the trigger. We didn't learn of our mistake until the next morning."

"Were you sorry?"

"I was worried. I admit we were scared. I was afraid we'd be caught any minute. We decided to leave America right away. That's why I took such risks to get Slobodin before we left. That night, we were hanging on the edge. But we were lucky." He was silent for a moment. "Slobodin did die, didn't he? I saw no mention of his death in the papers."

"Yes," Saunders said. "He is dead."

"The rifle we used is at the bottom of the Hudson. I can draw you its exact location if you want it. We had a rented car. Two hours after killing Slobodin, we were on our way back to Europe."

"But you didn't arrive together?"

"No. Christine came home on another plane, via Brussels. I wanted to keep her out of it as much as possible."

"You want her kept out of it even now?"

Luçot closed his eyes. "Yes, even now."

The church bells rang twice.

The night had taken on a nightmare quality—the dead man at the desk, the two sheets of paper written in blood, their terrible secret finally revealed, and the assassin standing motionless in front of him, all in black, his toneless recital in sharp contrast to the burning light in his eyes.

143

Saunders' mouth was dry and had a bitter taste. "Why didn't Christine go with you to Israel?"

"I didn't want her to. She didn't know about my relationship with Lev Jourbin. When I saw his name in the manuscript, I froze. If he'd been there then, I would have murdered him in cold blood. Afterwards, I thought it over. I wanted to be sure it was the same Jourbin. That's why I asked for his address at the Zentralstelle. Once I was really convinced, I decided to go and see him and explain to his face what I was doing. I could tell him the truth. And I knew he would tell me the truth."

"You told him everything?"

"Everything."

"What did he say?"

"He cried. He cried the whole night. He sat next to me, hugged me and sobbed like a child. He didn't mention my revenge, he said nothing when I told him how I'd killed them, one by one. He cried again when I told him that I intended to commit suicide after my mission was completed."

"Did he describe his part in your father's murder?"

Luçot nodded. "He told me how five men had pinned him to the ground while the others finished off my father. The screams that were heard in the adjoining blocks were his. My father didn't make a sound. He died right away. Jourbin said he was already dying when they started to attack him."

"How did Jourbin come out of it alive?"

"He was a Russian and an officer, so some of the prisoners were scared to touch him and they protected him from the others. He stayed on in the same block. You can imagine what it was like for him after that—living day after day, sleeping at night next to those monsters! That's when he swore he would do everything he could for me. My father had told him about me. He kept his promise."

"He drowned the day before yesterday."

"No, he didn't drown. He committed suicide. The shock was too much for him. That night we spent together he kept calling me 'my son'. His son the killer, the avenger; his son who had made him relive the terrible experience he had tried to bury for thirty years. It was too much for him."

"What did Christine think of this?"

"Christine? I didn't tell her. She thought I had gone to Israel to kill him."

There was a pause.

"How did you learn about me?"

"Christine. She saw you on the stairs when you came to search my apartment. She saw you leave and followed you. Then she tried to detain you by staging the accident on the Autoroute du Sud."

"But why? Jourbin was already dead and you were back in Paris."

Luçot shook his head. "No, you're wrong. She didn't know Jourbin was dead. I told her I needed three days in Israel and she did what she could to make sure no one interfered with me during those three days."

"I don't understand. If you needed three days, why were you back in Paris within twenty-four hours?"

"I wasn't. Look."

He pulled a newspaper clipping from his pocket. "It's from this morning's *Süddeutsche Zeitung*."

Saunders glanced at the paper and gasped. The headlines read: "Mysterious murder in Munich. The victim industrialist Hans Fischer, turns out to be a former S.S. officer and Nazi war criminal. Joakim Müller. The possibility of revenge by a survivor of the death camps is not excluded."

Saunders didn't bother to read the rest. He looked at Luçot. "So you found him?"

"Yes. I found him too."

Saunders was silent for a moment.

"You didn't have his address when you left for Israel?"

"That's right."

"You found it there?"

"No. I don't know if Schneider told you everything, but ever since my last trip to Vienna, I had been telephoning him every day to find out if the investigation on Müller had turned up anything. It was always 'no'. But two days ago, when I called him from Tel Aviv, he was very excited. He told me he had just received the information I wanted from an absolutely reliable source. He said Müller had assumed the name Hans Fischer and that his address was 17 Rizzastrasse, Munich. I decided to act right away. I said goodbye to Jourbin, took the Paris plane and got off at Munich. I was back in Paris this morning."

"You've done all this by yourself? All these murders without anyone finding out or even suspecting you?"

"You found out. But I already told you, all I cared about was having enough time. After that, it didn't matter."

"You think your mission is really accomplished?"

"What do you mean?" Luçot was suddenly anxious.

"There were fifteen names on your list. You've found only six, not counting the two who were already dead."

"Are there any more?" Luçot lunged at Saunders.

"No," Saunders said impassively. "But what happened to the others?"

Luçot let go of him. "You scared me. I thought maybe someone had escaped me. But you don't need to worry, Mr. Saunders. I checked every list. All the others died at Dachau. Dead, dead like dogs. They're all dead. Not a single one of those who touched Robert Luçot is alive—you hear, not one!"

"You are insane," Saunders said quietly.

"Yes, I'm a madman. But a madman who succeeded all the way."

"No, not all the way. There's Christine. She talked to me tonight. She asked me to tell you that she never wants to see you again."

This time, it hit home. Luçot crumbled, covering his face with his hands. "I don't understand. Why is she doing this? What happened? When I got back this morning, I called her from the airport. I was so happy. I told her that it would all be over tonight—when I had killed this monster, Cyrankiewitz. And I told her about my greatest triumph, that I had found Müller and killed him. I described it to her in detail; she didn't say a word. Then I don't know what happened but she suddenly cut me short and said: 'I don't ever want to see you again. You have ruined my life,' and hung up. That's what she said: 'You have ruined my life.' I tried all day to find her, at her apartment, at mine, at all the places we usually met. Nothing. She has disappeared."

"But what's the difference?" Saunders said coldly. "You intended to commit suicide, didn't you?"

Luçot looked at him as if he were coming out of a dream.

146

"Suicide? Yes, of course I intended to commit suicide. I kept telling her I would, and she agreed it was the only way. But she swore she would stay by me to the very end, to my end. Then all of a sudden, just like that ... I don't understand. By God, I don't understand!"

Luçot crouched before him, his head in his hands, sobbing. Saunders waited.

Finally Luçot looked up.

"I want to ask you just one thing. If you agree, I'll do whatever you ask."

Saunders nodded.

"Keep her out of this."

"But she's already in it."

"No, it isn't true. You had an accident. She side-swiped your car. These things happen. You talked to her on the telephone. I suppose she gave you this address. But none of that means anything. Maybe she simply wanted to stop the massacre.

"Just don't get her mixed up in this. Please. I did everything I could to keep her out of it. We were never seen together, not in any hotel, in any travel agency. We never registered together. I beg you ... She has suffered enough and because of this, she may suffer all the rest of her life. Leave her alone and I'll give you what you're after."

"What is that?"

"A signed confession, a detailed report of everything I did from the moment I received the manuscript of *Letters in Blood* to now. I will leave out only Christine's name and her part in it. All you're after is the solution to Ponomarev's murder—isn't that why you've been chasing me half-way around the globe? Don't worry, Mr. Saunders. I will tell the whole truth in my confession. 'The mistaken murder of Ponomarev.' And that will certainly put you in line for a promotion..."

At three fifty-three on September 1st, a single shot rang through the second floor of 75 Rue Chautemps in Montmartre. Saunders, still bound to his chair, had no illusions as to what it meant.

But it wasn't until two hours later, as a sad grey dawn

147

began to settle over Paris, that the police arrived and freed Saunders. In the adjoining room, they found Jean-Marc Luçot stretched out on the bed, still holding a revolver against his smashed temple. In his other hand was a sheaf of papers covered with fine handwriting—the history of his vendetta.

Saunders looked at him for a long time, feeling neither satisfaction nor relief. To be sure, his mission was accomplished. Luçot had kept his promise. The proof that Ponomarev had been killed accidentally was there, clutched in the dead man's hand. There would be no war, Saunders would reap the fruits of his success, and yet it all seemed a hollow victory. He felt deeply depressed, and he didn't know whether the depression was caused by the thought of all Luçot's victims, or of the doomed Luçot himself.

He walked down the stairs and into the street. Paris was waking up and shaking off its morning mists. He lit a panatella, and asked the police officer who had followed him: "How did you happen to arrive at the right place at the right time?"

The officer smiled: "An anonymous telephone call. A woman's voice, I believe. It happens quite often, you know. People hear or see something, but they don't want to get involved. So they call us and go back to sleep with a clear conscience."

"Not always," Jeff said, inhaling deeply. "Not always."

10

BERNIE PRENTISS, THE VETERAN A.P. CORRESPONDENT, HAD the first flash on the teletype at ten seventeen that morning. "Mystery Ponomarev murder solved. Killed by mistake by young Frenchman. Killer committed suicide leaving full confession. More coming."

Two minutes later, it was the U.P.'s turn; Reuters joined in at ten twenty-six at the same time that Agence France Presse was giving a run-down of the story. Even Tass showed unaccustomed speed, cabling the news to Moscow at ten thirty-seven.

Then came the deluge.

At ten forty-two, Laurent Ribaud, the information director for Channel Europe 1 burst into the studio on Rue François Premier and broke into *Pour Vous Madame* with a voice that trembled with emotion. Radio Luxembourg was first with an interview with the police officer who discovered Luçot's body. France-Inter interrupted its broadcasts with dramatic readings of Luçot's confession. *Le Figaro* and *France-Soir* swamped Paris with thousands of copies of special editions carrying the first photographs and stories. *Le Monde* broke tradition and printed on its front page a photocopy of that part of the confession where Luçot described how he accidentally shot Ponomarev.

The tidal wave engulfed Europe, America, Asia. Radio and television stations across the world interrupted their regular broadcasts. Tens of thousands of newspapers printed special editions. Journalists, reporters and television crews invaded

Paris. Descending on Vienna, on the Zentralstelle, on South Africa and Israel, journalists retraced Luçot's "trail of blood" from the time he left Editions Fontenoy, to 75 Rue Chautemps on the Butte Montmartre. For two weeks, the world talked of nothing but the "avenger" and his "tragic destiny".

In Moscow, for the first time since the Bolshevik Revolution, *Pravda* published a special edition. From East to West, the world was caught in a wave of emotion unmatched since John Kennedy's assassination. Even though the story of Luçot, assassin and victim at the same time, was horrifying, everyone felt an enormous sense of relief. War between the United States and the U.S.S.R. had been averted. The President of the U.S.A. and Prime Minister Kuznietzov congratulated each other over the "hot line", and promised to have an early summit meeting to discuss means of avoiding future misunderstandings. The Red Army alert was lifted and thousands of soldiers on leave flooded the streets of Moscow. In the United States, students hungry for peace organised spontaneous demonstrations on campuses throughout the country. In Rome, groups of young people overcome with enthusiasm danced and sang to the glory of peace in front of the Soviet Embassy. Only one man, Rod Gilpatrick of the London *Times*, reminded his readers that "the world is celebrating against the backdrop of one of the ghastliest tragedies since the beginning of time". But few paid him any heed. The personal tragedy of Jean-Marc Luçot was quickly forgotten. What mattered was that the peace was preserved. Only the more sensational aspects of "the Luçot affair" still made an occasional column.

But jubilation was not entirely universal. The *Red Flag,* organ of the Red Army, sulked in stubborn silence. Its tirades against "the instigators of imperialist wars and the assassins of Ponomarev" had mis-fired. On the other hand, the *People's Daily* in Peking, uninhibited as usual by any scruples about veracity, announced that Luçot was nothing but "a mercenary, hired by the forces of reaction and revisionism to assassinate Soviet Minister Ponomarev under the pretext of a false story of revenge concocted by bourgeois capitalists".

Christine de La Maleyne's name never once appeared in print. The French authorities had no desire to see more

French nationals mixed up in the affair. The police had removed the girl's photograph from Luçot's apartment, along with all other indications of her presence there. Christine herself had disappeared from her studio on the Rue Mirabeau and no one knew her whereabouts.

Another name left unmentioned was Jeff Saunders'. A few telephone calls from Jim Sullivan and Hal Richards to their French colleagues made certain he would be kept out of it, even though the two chiefs had to listen to several choicely worded criticisms of their "clandestine activities in a friendly capital".

While the story broke, Jeff Saunders slept the sleep of the just in his room at the George V in Paris. His slumbers were interrupted twice: first, by a call from Hal Richards congratulating him on his success and assuring him that he would be "suitably rewarded for the courage and devotion with which you have accomplished your mission". The second call was from the President of the United States informing him that it was his privilege to accord him the Intelligence Medal, one of the highest decorations in the land. Saunders mumbled a few words of thanks, hung up and went back to sleep.

He didn't wake up until eight thirty that night. It was another telephone call. A gentle female voice wished to remind him that he was the guest of honour that night at a private dinner at the United States Embassy. Five minutes later it was Jim Sullivan. By now he was done with the emotion and praise he had lavished on him when Saunders woke him with the news of Luçot's suicide. All he said was: "Jeff, I'll stop by for you at nine o'clock. I hope this gives you enough time to get dressed. The Ambassador is very fussy about punctuality, you know. He doesn't like people to be late."

Saunders muttered something into the receiver and crawled painfully from under the covers. A cold shower, a shave and two glasses of whisky brought him back to reality. He glanced out of the window. A heavy autumn rain was falling.

The telephone rang again to announce that Jim Sullivan

151

was waiting downstairs. He had almost finished dressing. He went through the pockets of the suit he had worn the day before to transfer wallet, comb, cigars into his fresh suit. His hand felt something stiff in the inside breast pocket: it was the envelope containing the documents and the photograph he had "borrowed" from the Zentralstelle, the copies of the documents that had been sent to Luçot. As he absentmindedly looked through them, he suddenly felt his blood turn to ice. He picked up the phone and dialled three different numbers before he got an answer.

"Is this Mademoiselle Leroy?" he said hoarsely.

The familiar prim voice at the other end said: "Yes."

He asked her several questions; she asked him to wait a few moments: she would have to call the office on the other phone. The minutes seemed endless. He bit his nails, tried in vain to light a panatella and noted with shame the trembling of his hands.

Finally, Mademoiselle Leroy was back. She seemed a little surprised. He listened with attention, thanked her and carefully returned the receiver to its cradle. His face was drained, and two deep furrows lined either side of his mouth. Then he grabbed his raincoat and ran for the elevator.

Jim Sullivan was waiting in the lobby.

"Hi, Jeff..."

Saunders cut him off: "Listen, Jim, something unexpected has turned up. I've got to leave right away."

"Leave? For where? What about the Ambassador?"

"Please give my apologies to the Ambassador. This is much more important."

And he ran out into the street leaving an outraged Sullivan behind. The D.S. was waiting. He slipped ten francs to the boy who had delivered the car and slid behind the wheel. Nervously he pumped the accelerator, the motor roared and he set off into the night and the driving rain.

The lights of Paris were far behind him now as the car sped down the rain-soaked road towards the south-west. Around him, sheets of rain alternated with bombardments of hail. The wind bent the trees double and blinding flashes of lightning bathed the countryside with a white light, picking out the broken branches by the side of the road. The narrow highway was virtually deserted.

He shot through Chartres with barely a glance at the towers of the cathedral looming black and impassive in the storm. At Châteaudun, he almost ran over a frightened policeman dashing across the street, his comical cape flapping in the wind. Saunders' weariness had vanished. He was tense, leaning alertly over the wheel and chewing on a succession of panatellas. He turned on the car radio.

"...in the Foreign Legion where he distinguished himself by his heroism and courage, but also by a tendency to hold himself aloof, one of the most characteristic symptoms of paranoia. We have here in the studio his former commanding officer, Colonel Jean Bossigli. Colonel, would you share with our listeners your impressions of Jean-Marc Luçot as you remember him?"

"To be quite frank, I always thought Luçot was mad. The way he behaved, the way he threw himself into the midst of danger, convinced me that I was dealing with a madman..."

Jeff turned off the foxy old Colonel. He tried one station after another. Always the same thing: Jean-Marc Luçot's revenge. He gave up and concentrated on his driving. When he reached Tours, he dragged an irate old man from his bed to get his tank filled. The old man muttered about the dark, the storm, the rain and idiots who drove around in such weather. At Saumur—he had been driving for three and a half hours by then—he turned off the Route Nationale and headed south towards Bressuire. He was now on a local road in almost deserted country. It was pitch black and the windshield wipers couldn't keep up with the downpour. Suddenly there was a bolt of lightning and he saw it in all its savage splendour—the Château de Belvoir: the formidable ramparts with their crenellated towers; the deep moat, the heavy drawbridge with its thick chains, and finally the castle itself, a harmonious grouping of picturesque towers and pointed roofs.

The car bounced over the rough bridge, careered through the vast portal cut into the stone wall and came to a stop at the foot of the majestic stairway that led up to the main entrance.

He jumped out and ran up the stairs. The heavy door of carved oak was slightly ajar, letting in the wind which moaned and sighed in the vast deserted hall. Saunders went over to a small door on which a sign said "Private, No Entry", opened it and found himself in a long silent corridor. He turned on his flashlight and saw a narrow flight of stairs leading to the second floor. Another corridor—this one carpeted, muffling the sound of his footsteps—led into another large hall. Heavy curtains framed the windows, a crystal chandelier hung from the ceiling and tinkled in the wind. Only one of the double doors was open.

Saunders hesitated for a second, then walked in. The room was in almost complete darkness except for a rectangle of light opposite the door. The window was open, framing a lake that shimmered in the lightning's reflection.

She was standing exactly as he remembered her—motionless, by an open window.

"I knew you would come," she said.

He held his distance.

"I haven't come for what you think."

"You don't know what I think, Jeff."

"I came because of him."

"Yes, I know."

"He asked me not to involve you."

She shrugged. "What difference does it make? You can run away from people, you can run away from Paris and lock yourself up. But, the old saying is right, you can't run away from your memories."

"Nor from the truth, Chris," he said quietly.

She said nothing.

"Sometimes, after a superhuman effort, you think you've found the truth. You're sure it's the truth, the whole truth and nothing but the truth. Then, all of a sudden, a new light falls on the picture and reveals things you hadn't noticed before. And you realise that what you thought was the truth was a lie, a *trompe l'oeil*, an optical illusion. And behind that optical illusion is another truth. A second truth, and maybe even a third truth."

"And you've come to tell me the other truth?"

154

"Yes. Do you want to hear it?"

Again she made no reply.

"Last night, before Jean-Marc shot himself, we had a long, long talk. I asked him how he found out Slobodin's address in New York, since none of the people he had contacted knew Slobodin was the chauffeur for the Soviet U.N. delegation. Jean-Marc told me that you had gone to the Zentralstelle, and that with the help of a group of East European refugees, they found you Slobodin's address.

"Now I was at the Zentralstelle, Chris, and I have all the documents they assembled for Jean-Marc's investigation. You were never at the Zentralstelle, Chris, and no such group ever gave them Slobodin's address. Who gave you that address, Chris?"

She still said nothing.

"Last night, I asked Jean-Marc how you found me, how you knew I was following you, why you tried to keep me from leaving Paris with your clever little accident. He said you had seen me entering his apartment.

"Now I wasn't alone in that apartment. There were six of us. How did you know which one to follow? How did you know I was the agent who was after Luçot? How did you know I was the one you had to detain even at the risk of causing a serious accident? Who told you I was the dangerous man, Chris?"

Still no word.

"Jean-Marc told me that you encouraged him when he dreamed up the idea of revenge, that you supported and helped him, that you were devoted to him body and soul. And that you swore to stay by him to the very end. He also said that you approved of his idea of committing suicide when his revenge was accomplished. You spent large sums of money on his project. Why did you do it, Chris? For love? I don't believe it. You're a beautiful girl, you've always had armies of handsome rich young men following you around. Why should you fall in love with this poor unhinged loner?

"You'd known Jean-Marc from his lectures on the Résistance. Your father was a member of the Résistance who had been killed by the Nazis. That is why you were attracted to

155

him; you had something in common. That's what you told him, isn't it, Chris?

"Three hours ago, I made a telephone call to find out the truth. And the truth is very different, Chris. Your father was not a member of the Résistance. Your father was a fascist, a collaborator. During the war, General Von Braunschwig set up his headquarters here in this very castle at your father's invitation. Yes, your father was indeed executed. But not by the Nazis. By the Résistance and for treason.

"Jean-Marc may have shot Slobodin, Dragner, Ponomarev, Brajinski, Talbot and the rest . . he was the one who pulled the trigger. But he wasn't the true murderer. You made him do it and in diabolical cold blood. You are the real murderer, Chris."

There was a long silence.

"You have nothing to say?"

There was a rumble of thunder and a burst of rain blew in the open window.

She turned slowly towards him.

"Everything you say is true, Jeff. He pulled the trigger but I am the real murderer."

Then she began to talk, rapidly, in a low voice. Occasionally it dropped to a whisper and Jeff had to strain to hear her. From time to time, she turned away to look out of the window.

"Last February, I went to St. Moritz for two weeks of skiing. I needed a rest; I was exhausted from moving from one apartment to another and ... and a love affair had gone on the rocks. I stayed where I usually do, at the Hotel des Grisons. A few days after I arrived, I met a man named Kurt. Or I should say, he ran into me as I was coming down a trail. We got into conversation—we could hardly help it. He turned out to be a German, from West Berlin, and an expert on economics and political science. He had an important job doing research in a think-tank attached to the Bonn government. Of course, I didn't know any of that at the start. All I knew was that he was the most charming man I had ever met."

With nervous steps, she went over to a small table, picked

156

don't. You were right about my father. I never knew him but I grew up in the shadow of the things people said about him. I learned to hate the Communists with a passion. And I never hated the Germans. My father was a noble man. If he helped the Germans, he must have had good reasons for it.

"But none of that matters. We were in Corfu when Kurt told me about his father. He talked for hours. He said he loved me more than life itself, and by then I knew it. He told me how much he wanted to marry me. But he couldn't. There was a terrible curse on his family. His father had been an S.S. officer at the concentration camp at Dachau. He was a good law abiding man who had never lifted a finger against the prisoners in his charge. On the contrary, he had tried to save a number of them. There was a war going on, he understood that, and he knew that terrible things happen during all wars. But he himself never did anything wrong. Only one night, he had the misfortune to witness an unspeakable incident: a group of prisoners—some of them already completely mad—killed one of the prisoners and ... tore him to pieces. I was appalled when I heard it. Kurt's father had been appalled too, but his pity for the miserable wretches kept him from reporting the incident. If he had, the fifteen prisoners would certainly have been executed.

"But that turned out to be a serious mistake, because the band of assassins soon realised there had been a witness, that someone knew what they had done. None of them, of course, would ever open his mouth, but Müller might. So they decided they must get rid of him, to reduce the only witness to their crime to silence. Immediately after the war, they testified before the American authorities. They described Joakim Müller as a blood-thirsty monster, a sadist who with studied refinement had tortured and killed hundreds of prisoners. Müller was forced to go into hiding under an assumed name. He lived in perpetual fear, knowing that the post-war climate in Germany and the world at large was such that no one would believe him; only the prisoners would be listened to.

"As for the prisoners themselves, they were afraid to go back to their countries in case someone discovered what had happened that night in Block 13. This was especially true of

158

the Russians. Only Slobodin returned to the Sovie[t] All the others emigrated to the West and scattere[d] was clear that if Joakim Müller ever showed his f[ace] would make common cause and stop at nothing to b[ring] to justice.

"So the real killers, who had murdered an innocen[t] ded Frenchman, went freely about their business. Th[at made] my blood boil.

"But then came the moment of truth. Kurt ha[d been] living a quiet, inconspicuous life; no one showed any [interest] in his origins, his name—Müller is one of the com[mon] names in Germany. Then suddenly, he was given hi[s big] chance: he was offered an important diplomatic post in [Wash-] ington. The German Foreign Minister considered hi[m one] of the coming stars in the diplomatic service and was [ready] to put his full weight behind Kurt's career.

"But Kurt knew that the minute his appointmen[t was] announced, the Americans and probably the German[s] would start digging around in his past. They woul[d dis-] cover that he was the son of Joakim Müller, the 'Sata[n' of] Dachau. The scandal would destroy him, he would be f[orced] to resign. Germany cannot allow herself to be repres[ented] abroad by the son of a Nazi criminal. But even worse, [they] would soon find out that he maintained close relations [with] one Hans Fischer in Munich. In no time they would re[alise] that Hans Fischer and Joakim Müller were one and the s[ame] man. So, it would be a double tragedy, for father and [his] son.

"With me, he saw the possibility of realising both [his] dreams, to have me and his career, at the same time. All [that] was necessary was to silence forever the survivors of Bl[ock] 13."

"You really believed all this?"

Christine looked at Saunders for the first time since [the] start of her recital.

"I believe it to this day, Jeff. I believe every word he e[ver] said. Kurt has never lied to me."

"And he asked you to help him 'silence the survivors'?"

"He asked me to leave him. But I offered to help. I kne[w] it was the price I would have to pay if I was going to kee[p]

159

up a cigarette and lit it. Then she returned to her place by the window and continued.

"He invited me out once, twice, three times. At first it was casual enough, although I made no attempt to hide the fact that I found him very attractive. Jeff, have you ever had a dream come true? Have you ever dreamt about somebody or something all your life and suddenly have it appear before you in the flesh? That's what happened to me. Kurt was my dream. My fairy-tale 'Prince Charming'. I never thought I could fall in love that way, with my whole soul. And when I realised he felt the same, I was the happiest woman alive. We'd known each other only a week and I was madly in love. I still am. One word from him and I'd do anything. *Anything.*

"I left my hotel, he left his, and we went off together. We travelled for three whole weeks. Switzerland, Italy, Greece, Corfu. I was drunk with the magic of it—what we did together, what we saw together. I was ready to do anything, anywhere, to keep him with me."

"What did he ask you to do?" Saunders had an instinctive dislike for sentimental outpourings; he wanted to get her back on the subject.

"He didn't ask me to do anything. Or rather, just one thing. He asked me to marry him."

For the first time, Saunders felt a certain surprise. "He wanted to marry you? Did you accept?"

"Yes, he asked me to marry him and I accepted. I won't tell you how I felt at that moment. But the minute I accepted, it was clear that it could never happen."

Saunders waited.

"I told you his name was Kurt. But I didn't tell you his family name. It was Müller. His name was Kurt Müller. Does the name Müller mean anything to you, Jeff?"

"Müller?" A shiver ran through him. "He was the son of Joakim Müller? I don't believe it!"

"Yes. He was Joakim Müller's son."

There was a pause, then Chris continued.

"Of course I had no idea who Joakim Müller was then. I didn't know or care. I wanted Kurt—that's all that mattered. I never believed all those stories about Nazi crimes and I still

157

don't. You were right about my father. I never knew him but I grew up in the shadow of the things people said about him. I learned to hate the Communists with a passion. And I never hated the Germans. My father was a noble man. If he helped the Germans, he must have had good reasons for it.

"But none of that matters. We were in Corfu when Kurt told me about his father. He talked for hours. He said he loved me more than life itself, and by then I knew it. He told me how much he wanted to marry me. But he couldn't. There was a terrible curse on his family. His father had been an S.S. officer at the concentration camp at Dachau. He was a good law abiding man who had never lifted a finger against the prisoners in his charge. On the contrary, he had tried to save a number of them. There was a war going on, he understood that, and he knew that terrible things happen during all wars. But he himself never did anything wrong. Only one night, he had the misfortune to witness an unspeakable incident: a group of prisoners—some of them already completely mad—killed one of the prisoners and ... tore him to pieces. I was appalled when I heard it. Kurt's father had been appalled too, but his pity for the miserable wretches kept him from reporting the incident. If he had, the fifteen prisoners would certainly have been executed.

"But that turned out to be a serious mistake, because the band of assassins soon realised there had been a witness, that someone knew what they had done. None of them, of course, would ever open his mouth, but Müller might. So they decided they must get rid of him, to reduce the only witness to their crime to silence. Immediately after the war, they testified before the American authorities. They described Joakim Müller as a blood-thirsty monster, a sadist who with studied refinement had tortured and killed hundreds of prisoners. Müller was forced to go into hiding under an assumed name. He lived in perpetual fear, knowing that the post-war climate in Germany and the world at large was such that no one would believe him; only the prisoners would be listened to.

"As for the prisoners themselves, they were afraid to go back to their countries in case someone discovered what had happened that night in Block 13. This was especially true of the Russians. Only Slobodin returned to the Soviet Union. All the others emigrated to the West and scattered. But it was clear that if Joakim Müller ever showed his face, they would make common cause and stop at nothing to bring him to justice.

"So the real killers, who had murdered an innocent wounded Frenchman, went freely about their business. That made my blood boil.

"But then came the moment of truth. Kurt had been living a quiet, inconspicuous life; no one showed any interest in his origins, his name—Müller is one of the commonest names in Germany. Then suddenly, he was given his great chance: he was offered an important diplomatic post in Washington. The German Foreign Minister considered him one of the coming stars in the diplomatic service and was ready to put his full weight behind Kurt's career.

"But Kurt knew that the minute his appointment was announced, the Americans and probably the Germans too, would start digging around in his past. They would discover that he was the son of Joakim Müller, the 'Satan' of Dachau. The scandal would destroy him, he would be forced to resign. Germany cannot allow herself to be represented abroad by the son of a Nazi criminal. But even worse, they would soon find out that he maintained close relations with one Hans Fischer in Munich. In no time they would realise that Hans Fischer and Joakim Müller were one and the same man. So, it would be a double tragedy, for father and for son.

"With me, he saw the possibility of realising both his dreams, to have me and his career, at the same time. All that was necessary was to silence forever the survivors of Block 13."

"You really believed all this?"

Christine looked at Saunders for the first time since the start of her recital.

"I believe it to this day, Jeff. I believe every word he ever said. Kurt has never lied to me."

"And he asked you to help him 'silence the survivors'?"

"He asked me to leave him. But I offered to help. I knew it was the price I would have to pay if I was going to keep him. And to keep Kurt, I was ready to pay *any* price."

"What did he say?"

"He explained how he thought to go about it. He had been in touch with a secret organisation that had helped his father escape and find a haven; it was still active and often helped former Nazi officers when they were in trouble. They said they would give him all the help he needed but refused to raise a finger against any former prisoners. Not only because the idea of murder was repugnant to them but also because they would be among the first to be suspected. It would be virtually impossible for anyone taking part in five or six murders not to be discovered. This would be a disaster for the organisation on which so many thousands of people depended.

"So, it was during one of their secret sessions that someone hit on the idea that the person who had the best motive to kill all those men was the victim's son, Jean-Marc Luçot. They knew he existed. They figured that the world would understand his motive and forgive him. The whole thing could be presented as a case of poetic justice—the son's revenge against his father's killers. They promised to put their worldwide network of agents at Luçot's disposal. But they also knew that Luçot would need someone to keep him at it, to encourage him, provide him with support—financial and otherwise—until he had killed every last one of his father's murderers."

"And they chose you."

"No," Christine corrected him, "I volunteered."

Outside, the storm was abating. From time to time, the clouds parted and a shaft of moonlight cast a macabre light on the castle, the lake, and on Christine's face as she stood by the window.

"I suppose they had *Letters in Blood* right from the start," Saunders said.

"Yes. Even before the end of the war, an S.S. officer had found the manuscript under the floor of a barracks which was being repaired. They kept it along with many other documents. Now was their chance to put it to use as a goad to Luçot's revenge."

Saunders knew the script by heart: "They got the manuscript into the hands of a publishing house in Munich which then dispatched it to Editions Fontenoy in Paris where it inevitably reached Jean-Marc. And Jean-Marc was off and running. He now knew the terrible truth about his father's death. He wanted to commit suicide, but you were already there. Right?"

"Yes, I was there."

"You planned all along to become Luçot's mistress?"

"I told you I was ready to do anything. By the end of February, I was back in Paris. Kurt's friends gave me all the information I needed."

"Did Kurt help too?"

"Absolutely not. We agreed that we must not see each other or have any contacts until the operation was over. It was essential that no one suspect even the slightest connection between us or our plan was doomed."

"So what happened after you got back to Paris?"

"They told me where I could meet Luçot. I went to one of his lectures, told him I was interested in his ideas, that I was the daughter of an old Résistance fighter. He didn't dare ask me for a date so I had to take the initiative, pretending I wanted to hear more about the Occupation. Finally, he got up the nerve to ask for what he wanted. It didn't take too much effort since I was more than ready."

"And after he got the manuscript you encouraged him in his suicide idea?"

"Yes, it was part of the plan. He was supposed to disappear once the operation was completed."

"The money you needed came from the 'organisation', I take it?"

"Yes, most of it. They have vast financial resources. The men who work for the organisation are extremely clever. I spent a week in Hamburg learning their methods before I returned to Paris. Wherever we went, there were always a dozen people ready to help me. And I rarely met the same person twice during the operation. Their system was really amazing."

"Was it you who prodded Luçot to go and see Schneider in Vienna and the Zentralstelle?"

"No, I didn't need to. The moment he decided to seek his

revenge, he was more eager even than I. When he came back to Paris, he told me about everything he'd found out. I realised that he was lacking just two things: Slobodin's address and Müller's. I was convinced he would never find Müller. I pretended to go to Ludwigsburg to find Slobodin's address, but actually I stayed right here, for three days. Kurt and his father's friends have far more information than the Zentralstelle. They knew Slobodin was the chauffeur for the Soviet delegation in New York and they had his home address."

"How many of the trips did you make with Jean-Marc?"

"I went to Lyon for Michel Talbot. But in Lyon and Capetown, my role was purely passive. All I had to do was alert a few people to make sure the police didn't arrive before we had time to get away—all this without Jean-Marc's knowledge, of course. In the United States, I was much more active. I received detailed instructions by phone each day. It was Kurt's friends who set the day and hour for Steven Dragner's murder in Miami Beach. Also, the day and hour of Slobodin's."

"What do you mean?" Saunders' attention was suddenly very sharp.

"They were very strict with me in America. They told me exactly when I was to leave New York and where I was to go. Jean-Marc had started following Slobodin, but he was only an amateur. There were several times when he wanted to shoot him then and there and I always had to hold him back until I got the green light. Our men saw Slobodin leave the delegation headquarters alone in the car. They phoned me that the time was ripe but that it would be better to wait until later that night. You know the rest: we followed him to the service entrance of the Plaza, we saw him get out of the car, then return and leave the city. In the dark, neither of us could see well enough to know that the man getting into the car was not the same one who had got out. So we followed him, waited, and shot him. We didn't realise our mistake until the next morning. That was the only mistake in the whole operation. Jean-Marc wanted to wait a few days before we had another try at Slobodin, but Kurt's friends ordered me to put the pressure on him to do the job and get out. I realised later that they were right. If we had waited, we would never have been able to kill Slobodin."

"Why didn't you go with him to Israel?"

"Because he made it very clear that he didn't want me to. I didn't know he had been friends with that Jew—Lev Jourbin—for such a long time. Anyway, he was so insistent that I had to give in. Besides, I had a job to do in Paris: to detain you."

"How did you know about me?"

"We spotted you in Vienna and again in Ludwigsburg; by the time you got to Paris, we knew all about you."

"What were your orders? To kill me?"

"Certainly not! I wouldn't have done it in any case. They only wanted me to hold you for a few hours so that Jean-Marc could do his job in Israel. I'm afraid I did you more harm than I meant to. All I had in mind was a gentle collision —just enough to make you miss your plane."

"Then it was you who told Jean-Marc about the Pole's being in Paris?"

"Yes. It was a matter of routine checking with a Polish refugee group. I learned through them that Cyrankiewitz had been living in Paris for years. The error in the Zentralstelle files was caused by the fact that his family in Lodz had written to the Red Cross in his name so that they could receive his pension and food parcels."

"And is that the whole story?"

"That is the whole story."

There was another long pause. Finally Saunders said: "I think you've overlooked a few things, Chris. What went wrong? Why are you here? Why did you leave Luçot? Why did you try to reach me at Le Bourget? What made you suddenly care whether Cyrankiewitz lived or died? Why did you try to save his life?"

She turned towards him. Even in the dark, he could see that her eyes were filled with tears; she suddenly looked like a wounded animal.

"I know that Jean-Marc was telephoning Schneider every day to see if he had found out Müller's address—Kurt's father's address. That didn't worry me too much. I was convinced he would never find him. How could I know that it would happen just when he was in Israel—out of my reach?

I still don't understand how Schneider got the address at the very moment when we were within sight of our goal. It was the first time that Jean-Marc did anything without my knowing. He got off the plane at Munich and killed Kurt's father."

"So everything was over?"

"When Jean-Marc called me from Orly he was wild with excitement. He told me he had found 'Satan' and that he had killed him. I didn't understand at first, then it came to me: he had found Joakim Müller and killed him. He had wrecked everything. I realised right away that it was all over for me, that I would never see Kurt again."

"What happened after that?"

"Exactly what I expected. I had a call from Berlin. I heard Kurt's voice. He said: 'Listen to me and don't you speak. I trusted you; I placed my life, my future in your hands. You have betrayed me. You have brought me disaster. I am finished. My father's body lies in the morgue and his picture is in all the papers. He is dead; I am dead. I never want to see you again.'"

Saunders felt a pang, almost of pity, for this girl whose dreams had been shattered.

"When Kurt hung up, I felt I was going mad. I called one of our liaison men in Paris, one I'd talked to over and over again. He said: 'Avoid all further contact with us. You will never see Kurt again; you will never see us.' That was when I suddenly felt horror at the thought of all those murders—the useless massacre. So I called you. I thought at least I could prevent one last killing. And I asked you to tell Jean-Marc that I never wanted to see him again."

She was silent and turned away again, towards the moon-lit lake and the forest of chestnuts that stretched to the far horizon. The tears she had held back so long began to roll down her cheeks. There was nothing to say. He let out a deep sigh and was about to leave the room when she spoke once more: "Jeff."

He stopped.

"I probably won't ever see you again either. I just wanted you to know ... that night after the accident..." Her voice became timid like a small girl's: "Once I saw that you were all right, after the accident ... there was no need for me to stay. I could have left. But I took you back to the hotel and stayed with you ... It wasn't necessary. It wasn't in the plan, you know."

"Really?" Saunders said evenly and left the room, his steps echoing down the marble floors of the Château de Belvoir.

11

It was five thirty in the morning when Saunders got back to his hotel room. The heavy curtains had not been drawn and in the first pale light of dawn filtering into the room, his haggard glance fell on Jim Sullivan asleep in a chair by the window. Saunders shook him gently.

Sullivan started. "What is it? Who..." Then he recognised the familiar face leaning over him. "You're back! Thank God. Where the hell have you been?"

"I'll tell you later. But just what are you doing here?"

Sullivan was wide awake now. "We were worried about you. We didn't know where you'd gone. The chief said I was to find you and tell you to get in touch with him."

"The chief? Did you call Hal Richards just because I didn't go to the Ambassador's dinner?"

"It was Hal who called me. He wanted to talk to you. He was wild when he learned you'd disappeared. I haven't heard him carry on like that in years."

Jeff threw his wrinkled jacket on the bed, loosened his tie and unbuttoned his shirt. Exhausted, he sat down on the edge of the bed.

"What's he mad about?"

"I don't know. He's trying to find you. I had a hard time explaining that you'd lit off and I had no way of following you. Where did you go, Jeff?"

"I went to see Christine de La Maleyne."

Sullivan let out a juicy expletive. "You're not going to tell me it was because you wanted to spend another night with

166

her? A repeat of the touching scene at the Orly Hilton? Perhaps you had another accident, and the young lady saved you once again? The head of the C.I.A. is looking for you all over France and you . . . you . . ."

"Calm down, calm down." He was too tired to listen to Sullivan's indignation. "Listen, Jim. I learned some things that have completely upset all our theories."

"What do you mean? What did you learn?"

"I haven't got the energy to tell the story twice. Get Hal on the phone and you listen in."

Sullivan pulled the telephone towards him and dialled. "While we wait, cast an eye on this." And he handed Saunders the sheaf of papers he was clutching.

Saunders passed a weary hand over his unshaven face and glanced with indifference at the mass of telegrams in his hands. They all carried the heading of the American Embassy telegraphic service and the signature of the decoder. They were telegrams of congratulations from C.I.A. chiefs, from Bill Pattison, from the head of the F.B.I., from the Secretary of State, and—most profuse of all—a long telegram from Hal Richards. But outdoing even Hal Richards was the one from the President of the United States, which contained every superlative in the book. The only one that got past his massive indifference was the Soviet Prime Minister's message to the President of the United States: he wished to extend his thanks to "all the anonymous men in your country who, thanks to their efficient and dedicated work, succeeded in solving the problem of this tragic mystery, thus re-establishing the friendship and understanding between our two countries."

"That should be framed and put on display at headquarters. The head of the Soviet government congratulates Uncle Sam's secret agents on their remarkable performance. Can you believe it?"

Sullivan was busy with the phone. "Ah, here we are. Hal? Hal? It's Jim here, in Paris. Our friend is back. He's ready to talk to you. Yes, he's right here."

Jeff took the receiver. "Hal? Good morning—or rather . . . What time is it with you?"

"Jeff, my boy . . ." It had to be something special to warrant

167

this term of affection. "Where in Christ's name have you been? You had us worried."

"Listen carefully now, Hal." And Saunders started slowly, weighing each word. "I had a sudden idea last night and I had to go and check it out."

"Check out what?" Richards' voice sounded apprehensive.

"I went to see the girl friend of ... of our boy ... the one who finished his project and ... left for good. You know who I mean?"

"Yes, yes. But what got into you to go on checking things. The mission is over, terminated."

"Not exactly, Hal. I've discovered some new facts that cast an entirely new light on the story. It turns out that there is a third element in the situation. I found out some amazing things..."

"O.K. O.K.," Richards said with impatience. "Tell me all about it when you get back to Washington. I want you to take the first plane home and come straight here. There must be one within an hour or two."

"I can't, Hal." He didn't like his boss's tone. "I want to finish the investigation. I still have a few things to look into. It won't take me more than a couple of days at the most."

"Out of the question!" Richards was really angry now. "You come back to Washington right now!"

"But what's the hurry, Hal? I said I'd discovered something new. I think this whole thing is covering up something much bigger than anything we imagined. Let me get to the bottom of it."

"There is nothing beyond what we already know. I want you here. We have no time to lose. The man in the White House expects you tonight. He wants to hear the whole thing from your own lips, then pin some damn medal on your chest. And I want a detailed report myself. Our friends ... those who were most concerned at the start ... also want you back immediately. Neither of us want your role in this revealed, and our French colleagues are beginning to ask searching questions about you. Every extra minute you spend in France—or Europe for that matter—brings me new headaches."

"O.K., Hal. Just give me twenty-four hours. Don't be so

168

damn stubborn. I'll leave tomorrow noon at the latest."

"Not an hour later, Jeff. That's an order. Understand? An order!"

Saunders' mouth tightened. "I can't hear you, Hal. I get a lot of static. The connection must have gone bad." Breathing hard, he slowly put down the receiver.

Sullivan looked at him with astonishment.

At nine a.m. sharp, Jeff walked into a phone booth and asked long distance for Bonn. He talked for about fifteen minutes and, glancing at his watch, scanned an Air France schedule. "O.K. Fourteen forty-five in the transit lounge at the Cologne airport. I'll be there," and he hung up.

His plane arrived in Cologne at two thirty and at precisely two forty-five a large fat man wearing a hat walked up to one of the gates marked "No Entry", took a small card from his pocket and waved it under the nose of the police officer guarding the area. The officer nodded and unhooked the chain across the passage.

The German went straight up to Saunders and shook his hand warmly. The two men sat down in a corner of the hall and talked quietly for almost an hour. Finally Saunders got up.

"Konrad I can't thank you enough."

"Nonsense," the German said with a deep laugh. "What's a small service like this between friends? You've done much more for me."

At four twenty, Saunders was in a plane again, this time bound for Vienna.

At seven o'clock he was knocking on Egon Schneider's door.

Schneider did not look happy to see his old friend. Without so much as a word, he closed the door and led Saunders up the creaking stairs to his office. He sat down behind his desk, took out a packet of tobacco, filled his pipe with studied care and lit it. The silence in the house indicated that Schneider's wife and children must be out. As if he had read Saunders' thoughts, he broke the silence:

"I sent Lynda and the children to her parents. She couldn't stand the sight of another reporter."

"Have there been that many?"

Schneider gave a nervous smile: "I didn't know there were so many reporters in the world. They swept through my house and the archives like a horde of locusts. They had to know everything—about Luçot, about Joakim Müller, about Block 13 ... They had to see all the personal reports on all the victims, and all the details on the atrocities committed at Dachau. God! I'll never understand how they can gorge themselves on those atrocities then use them as casual background material for newspaper stories!"

"Did you give them what they asked for?"

Schneider shook his head. "At first, I talked to one or two who seemed to be serious. But when the avalanche started, I sent them packing. I wasn't going to be a publicity agent for Dachau."

Schneider was silent once again. Then he looked at Saunders. "You were the leading actor in all this, weren't you? Your name never came up but I knew right away you were the one who'd found the key to this nasty business."

"More or less."

"A terrible thing. I couldn't sleep. I couldn't get Luçot's last visit out of my mind. My God! I was an accessory to his crimes! I was the one who furnished all the information that led to his 'success'."

"Don't be so hard on yourself, Egon. He could have found the information in lots of other places, at the Zentralstelle, at Yad Vachem in Jerusalem ... And in any case, how were you to know?"

"You could have warned me. You could have given me a hint when you were here."

"That isn't true. You know perfectly well I couldn't tell you anything. At that point, all I had were groundless suspicions. I couldn't believe that a man who'd left so many clues—as if on purpose—could possibly be the murderer. As a matter of fact, I had no suspicions at all when I was here."

Schneider looked stricken as he puffed on his pipe. Suddenly he blurted out: "What do you want to know now?"

"First of all, I want your advice. Did you know about the murder in Block 13?"

"No. I never heard one word about it. I knew of several

170

cases of cannibalism in the death camps, especially where the Nazis had systematically starved the prisoners. The story as described in the papers sounded perfectly plausible to me."

"Now I have another question. Perhaps you remember that during my most recent visit, a few days ago, you told me that just before Luçot's visit you had received a delegation from the Organisation of Former Internees in Berne."

"Yes. They worked in the archives for a week."

"Did you help them?"

Schneider looked at him with surprise. "Why shouldn't I? What was wrong with that? I took them to the archives in the Rathaus basement and showed them how to use the files. I spent a day or two with them and when I saw they could make out without me, I left."

Saunders took his notebook from his pocket and started turning its pages. "You know, I saw Luçot before his death."

"Before he shot himself?"

Saunders nodded. "I was in an adjoining room but I couldn't do anything about it."

Schneider made no comment.

"Luçot told me that you had given him Joakim Müller's alias and address three days before. Is that correct?"

Schneider grew pale. "That's right. Why not? When you came to see me, you said you had no suspicions about him. You didn't ask me to break off my dealings with him. He called me every morning to find out how my investigation on Müller was progressing. At his request I had contacted every group and individual who might know anything about Müller. I thought he simply wanted to expose him."

"How did you finally get on to Müller?"

"Now that you ask, it does seem strange to me. For thirty years, we didn't know a thing about Müller. And when Luçot came to see me, I told him I thought we had virtually no chance of ever finding him—that he was probably dead or had gone into hiding in South America or perhaps the Near East. There was also the possibility that he had taken an assumed name and, like thousands of former Nazis, had started a new life somewhere in Germany. But Luçot was so insistent that I promised him I would try my best to find out. But none of my investigations turned up anything. Then, the morning Luçot called me from Tel Aviv, I had just received a telegram. One moment—I have it here somewhere."

Schneider poked among the files heaped on his desk. "It must be around here somewhere. I received it less than a week ago." He kept mumbling to himself, and at the end of a few minutes, he had the familiar blue sheet in his hand. "Here it is. I'll read it to you: 'According to a reliable source, we have learned that Joakim Müller lives at 17 Rizzastrasse, Munich, under the name of Hans Fischer—repeat 17 Rizzastrasse Hans Fischer.'"

"Who signed the telegram?"

Schneider looked at the telegram again and said: "It is signed: Organisation of Former Internees, Berne." Slowly, he laid the telegram down on the table.

It was almost ten o'clock when Saunders stood up and got ready to go. "I'm sorry I have to leave you but I have to head back to Washington tonight. I would like to share my doubts about all this with you, but I can't. All I can say is that there is another angle to this business: another truth is hidden somewhere behind all this and I can't get at it." Then he said with studied care: "You've cleared up certain details and you've given me part of the answer. But there is still another aspect that I cannot fathom. I'd hoped to find the solution here but, unfortunately, I haven't."

Schneider gave him a friendly pat on the shoulder. "I hope you know that it's not because I didn't try."

"I know. I'm sorry. If only I could talk to you without having to weigh each word. I feel so alone in this thing, especially since everybody thinks the mystery is all cleared up."

He was about to go when he suddenly turned back. "You know, it's odd but I see very little resemblance between the war-time Sturmführer Müller and the present industrialist Hans Fischer. Are you entirely sure they are one and the same?" Then Saunders gave him a guilty smile. "You won't tell on me? I stole a photograph from the Zentralstelle."

He took the picture from his pocket and held it out to Schneider.

The Austrian laughed. "You stole that photo from the

Zentralstelle and I had it here all the time!"

"You mean you had a copy of this photo in your archives and didn't tell me?"

"It wasn't a copy. I had the original! The Zentralstelle copied my photograph twenty years ago. They must have forgotten it was mine and I forgot I had it. I only remembered it when the war-time pictures of Hans Fischer—I should say Joakim Müller—came out in the papers. You know, I keep my file of photographs here in the house because I was afraid the dampness of the Rathaus basement would be bad for them. When I saw that face in the newspapers, I knew I had seen it before. I went through my file of photographs and there it was! A photo of Müller with some of the inmates of Block 13. I have it here somewhere ... just a minute." And again, Schneider shuffled through the mound on his desk. "Ah, here it is!"

Saunders looked at the picture and froze.

"What is it?" Schneider looked at Saunders anxiously.

Saunders didn't answer. He was staring at the picture, then, his hand shaking, he took it over to a stronger light. He slowly took the copy out of his pocket and compared the two. He looked first at one, then at the other, rubbing his face with agitated fingers.

Schneider looked at the photographs over Saunders' shoulder. They were identical except for one small detail: the copy from the Zentralstelle showed Slobodin's stocky figure and large head; in Schneider's original, it was a totally different person—a tall, thin man with protruding ears. It was not Slobodin; it was somebody else.

Minutes passed before Saunders could take his eyes off the two photographs. He gave Schneider a bewildered look, and glanced at the pictures once more. Then he understood.

12

THE SWEET SMELL OF AN INDIAN SUMMER NIGHT HUNG OVER
Washington. A gentle breeze rustled the leaves in the trees.

"My, oh my," the driver said to Saunders as they crossed
the bridge over the Potomac. "It's the kind of night that
makes you feel fifteen years younger!" and he chuckled
softly to himself.

Saunders asked the driver to drop him off a few hundred
yards from the mammoth C.I.A. building. He paid him,
took off his jacket which he folded over his arm, loosened his
tie and the top button of his shirt. It really was an enchanting
night. The enormous weariness he'd been carrying so long
vanished. His step was almost light, and he felt a kind of
fatalistic indifference as he walked up to the big iron gate
at the main entrance.

As usual, all the lights were on. The lights were never
turned off at C.I.A. headquarters so that foreign agents would
not be able to tell how many people were still in the building. Those thousands of bulbs burning in the almost deserted building gave him the disagreeable sensation of being
spied upon in a phantom house by thousands of invisible
eyes.

He showed his pass to the guard at the door.

"Oh yes, Mr. Saunders. Mr. Richards asked me to take
you to him as soon as you arrived. He's been waiting for you
all evening."

Saunders nodded and set off after the guard.

Hal Richards was waiting for him outside his office, planted in the middle of the vast deserted corridor. In the brutal light, Jeff noticed for the first time that his boss's crew-cut was turning grey, though he still looked young for his age.

As he came abreast of Richards, the guard turned on his heels and the sound of his steps receded down the endless corridor.

Richards did not put out his hand. He looked Saunders up and down and said in cold fury: "You know what your kind of behaviour is called, you son-of-a-bitch? You disobeyed a superior's orders. I could bring you before the council. I want to tell you..."

"Change the record, Hal," Saunders cut him off. "Drop it. I know everything."

"You know ... what?" For the first time in his life, Saunders heard a note of fear in his boss's voice.

"You heard me. I know everything. The whole truth, Hal."

Richards' shoulders sagged; he looked suddenly tired. "Come, let's go into my office. I think we both need a drink."

As Saunders went through the door, he felt as if an eternity had passed since he was last in that room—the night just a few days ago when Hal had dragged him from his bed and asked him to find the truth. Well, he'd found it all right.

Richards poured some Scotch into two glasses and, trying to look relaxed, sat down behind his desk.

"O.K., Jeff. Speak up."

Saunders had been waiting so long for this moment that, as he started speaking, his voice sounded like someone else's, a voice from far away.

"The operation was perfectly conceived. It had to succeed. The idea was very clever, its execution almost faultless. But those who conceived it made a few mistakes."

He wet his lips with the Scotch. "They forgot they were dealing with people—human beings, not marionettes. It never occurred to them for instance that Christine de La Maleyne might develop certain feelings for me, the enemy agent. It never occurred to them that she might phone me at Le Bourget as I was about to leave for Poland and try to prevent a murder that was no longer of any use to her. And since they overlooked this human lapse, they never imagined that I might meet Jean-Marc Luçot while he was still alive.

175

According to their plan, I was supposed to discover his body stretched out on the bed, clutching the written confession to his breast. A striking scene, to be sure. The confession was designed to answer all the questions without my being able to ask any. But thanks to the distraught Christine, I arrived too early. I talked to Luçot and was able to ask him about some things that had been bothering me. His answers led me back to Christine and she revealed the second truth. This truth turned out to be far less watertight than the first. That second truth took me back to Schneider in Vienna. And there, in a forgotten file, I learned the third truth."

He pulled the two photographs of Müller and the prisoners in Block 13 from his pocket and threw them on Richards' desk. His boss didn't so much as glance at them.

"The photograph was another mistake. They were out for perfection; they almost made it. But how could they know the original was in Egon Schneider's files? Then they made an even worse mistake. It almost cost them the whole operation. Can you guess what mistake I mean, Hal?"

Richards spoke with heavy sarcasm. "Yes, Jeff, do tell me what the mistake was."

"You chose me for the job, Hal."

"I'm going to tell you a story, O.K.? A purely imaginary story, you understand, and you fill in the details."

Richards said nothing.

"All right, here we go. During the past few years, there have been developments on the international scene that have greatly alarmed the United States and the Soviet Union. I am speaking of course of the arms race and the growing sophistication of nuclear weaponry. The smallest incident could lead to a world war which would automatically mean the end of the world, or at least, the end of Western civilisation. Recently, the leaders of the two super-powers have started to make real attempts to avert such a holocaust. They were determined to resolve their differences and to limit the arms race so that their efforts and their money could go towards solving human needs. Both governments were for it. But they overlooked the Red Army. Over the same period of time, the Red Army had hardened its position, and as a

176

result of its great successes in the Near East and in South-east Asia, it was feeling its muscle. The military was opposed to any limitation of arms; in fact, it wanted a much more hard-nosed policy in all Soviet dealings with the West.

"O.K. so far? Now, the leading hawk in the Soviet Union and a good friend of the Red Army was the late Minister of Foreign Affairs, Lev Ponomarev. He made it his job to frustrate any rapprochement between Moscow and Washington, and to sabotage the coming Disarmament Conference at all costs. Gradually, the leaders of the two countries came to the conclusion that Ponomarev was the biggest single obstacle to the success of their plan. But how to get him out of the way?

"At this point, an idea began to germinate in the minds of the Russian and American secret services, who warmly supported their respective countries' civilian leaders. The idea, quite simply, was to kill Ponomarev. I have no idea who thought of it first or how the first contacts were made, but I would guess that the idea was born in Moscow with the K.G.B. acting as midwife. They probably sent someone over to see you, Hal, and how I'd love to have been in on that conversation!

"So it was agreed that Ponomarev had to be eliminated. But an ordinary murder had two strikes against it. First, the assassin was likely to be caught and the plot exposed. Secondly, Ponomarev was always surrounded by bodyguards. It was virtually impossible to get near him. I have an idea it was you, Hal—it's your kind of thing—who first thought up an 'accident': a fall off a cliff, a car not making a turn, a plane crash ... But the Russians probably told you it wasn't all that easy, and the Red Army was likely to be very suspicious. If I'm not mistaken, Ponomarev had already been in an automobile accident near Leningrad seven or eight months ago. It was a miracle he survived. I'm certain that had they conducted an investigation, they would have found the long arm of the K.G.B. in it somewhere. In any event, the heads of the Soviet secret service drew two conclusions from the accident: any thought of another accident must be dismissed out of hand, and any attempt on Ponomarev's life must be made outside Russia.

"That's why they came to you. They knew you wanted

Ponomarev out of the way just as much as they did. So out of your joint discussions came the idea of an assassination here. They knew there was only one place in the world where Ponomarev was without his bodyguard, where he was completely alone, arrived alone, left alone: the home of his mistress, Olga Kirilenko. And how lucky for everybody that Madame Kirilenko lived in a New Jersey suburb in the United States of America!

"The next problem was how? It was essential that the American government, or any American organisation, or any American citizen *not* be implicated in the murder. It was also essential to avoid a political motive. Therefore the murder must be committed by a foreigner, and the foreigner has to be ignorant of his victim's identity. He must act in good faith and be ready to confess all when the time came.

"I said: a foreigner acting in good faith. And that is how you arrived at the formula for the 'murder by mistake'."

This time it was Saunders who got up to refill the glasses. Richards took a big gulp, buried his chin in his fists and continued to fix his eyes on Saunders.

"Now, who should kill Ponomarev? And for what reason? I bet it was the Russians who came up with the answers.

"The 'murder by mistake' was fine, but how to set it up? You had to have a killer who was out to murder one man but ended up killing another by mistake—Ponomarev. Who could the intended victim be? In New York, who was the man always at Ponomarev's side? Why Arkadi Slobodin, Ambassador Gaidukov's chauffeur! He was the one who always delivered the car to the hotel so that the Foreign Minister could go to his nocturnal trysts with Olga Kirilenko. The murderer would have every good reason to make a mistake: when he saw the Ambassador's car in the dark, driven by a lone man, he had to assume it was Slobodin. Foolproof, wouldn't you say, Hal?"

"Go on," Richards said without changing position.

"So the real victim was chosen: Slobodin. But who on earth would ever want to kill Slobodin? The K.G.B. goes to work and looks up every scrap of evidence in the Moscow archives. Everything in Slobodin's dossier is gone over with

178

a fine-tooth comb and they come up with the operative fact: Slobodin was a prisoner at Dachau. Maybe, just maybe, they could find something in the Dachau files that would justify Slobodin's murder thirty years later. They are shot with luck. In the Dachau archives, the Russians discover the very thing: a manuscript found by Communist agents at the end of the war which the K.G.B. had preserved as possible evidence against any Nazi criminal who might turn up in an important government post. That manuscript was *Letters in Blood*. And in these letters, they find a description of a particularly blood-curdling incident that took place in Block 13 during the night of December 23rd-24th, 1944: the brutal murder of one Robert Luçot—a Frenchman—and the acts of cannibalism perpetrated by a group of Russians and Poles.

"The K.G.B. starts an investigation and finds that Robert Luçot had a son and that this son does not know how his father died. They also find out that the boy is full of complexes, unbalanced, that he lives in the past, deeply troubled by the mystery of his parents' death. To top it off, he is an excellent marksman. In other words, the ideal man for the project.

"Little by little, the project ripens. First, Luçot must learn the terrible truth about his father's death. Then the idea of revenge must be planted and nurtured. He must be incited to kill every man who took part in his father's murder. Somehow, Slobodin must figure among his potential victims so that he kills Ponomarev, thinking he has shot Slobodin.

"The time has come to sow the necessary clues. This takes some doing, for although Slobodin was indeed at Dachau at the time, he was not in Block 13 and therefore had nothing to do with Luçot's murder. The Organisation of Former Internees in Berne comes to the rescue. It is a handy front for the K.G.B. in matters of sabotage and subversion. Three of their members—no doubt top Soviet agents—go to see Egon Schneider and worm their way into his Rathaus files. They fake the documents in Slobodin's dossier and include him among the prisoners in Block 13.

"Then they move on to the Zentralstelle and doctor some more documents. Their great discovery there is a photograph of Sturmführer Joakim Müller surrounded by some of his prisoners. They touch it up, grafting Slobodin's head onto someone else's body. That was their second mistake. I remember how struck I was with the resemblance between the Slobodin in the photograph and his passport picture. Obviously the Russians didn't have an old photograph of Slobodin so they had to make do with a more recent one. They didn't realise—and Schneider had forgotten—that the original of the Müller picture was in Vienna.

"The Russians were very efficient. I don't know if you remember the report I made on my conversation with Inge Knutte, the young secretary at the Zentralstelle. She told me about a delegation from a group of former internees which had gone off with the documents and photos in order to make copies and 'had brought them back in three days'. Those were our friends—or rather, your friends.

"Next on the agenda was the touching up of *Letters in Blood*. The Russians 'improved' two pages: pages 93 and 94. I don't suppose they made any great changes except to insert Slobodin's name among those who killed Luçot's father. Maybe they heated up the style a little to add fuel to Luçot's resolve. End of first stage.

"I suppose it was at that point that they came to you and proposed the idea. You bought it and the two of you divided up the work: the Russians would take care of the murders and you would set up the investigation that would lead to unmasking the murderer. The fact that your little plot was going to cause the death of eight people didn't bother you at all. Most of them were poor unhappy souls anyway, dogged by an evil destiny. What people won't do for the peace of the world . . .

"The next step was to find a clever stage director who would see to it that Luçot acted his part, never missed a cue, never improvised. For this task you chose Christine de La Maleyne."

" 'Chris to my American friends,' " Saunders murmured with a hint of tenderness in his voice. "Poor kid. You destroyed her life with a real flair. Oh, the choice was inspired all right: beautiful, intelligent, an aristocrat from an extreme right-wing family and her father shot as a collaborator with the Nazis. Perfect. So you threw her into the arms of 'Kurt Müller'.

"Who was this Kurt Müller, Hal? Sure, I know he was a Soviet agent. First, because the story he told Chris was a lot of crap. I didn't believe a word of it. For another, we know that Joakim Müller didn't have a son.

"The Russians—as who doesn't—have several agents who play the professional Don Juan. Usually their job is to seduce the wives of Western V.I.P.s in the interests of blackmail. For this particular scheme, you got their most brilliant actor. It made me positively jealous, the way Chris described this Casanova. What a set-up! The slopes of St. Moritz, passionate love-making, the trip to Italy, Greece, Corfu ... Gives you goose-flesh, doesn't it? Then 'Kurt Müller' senses that credulous Christine is ripe for the Greek tragedy he is about to unfold. She swallows the whole bit, including the tabloid tales about secret Nazi organisations ready to arrange everything, pay for everything—who are, of course, our friends the K.G.B. Chris volunteers immediately and takes on the job of inciting Luçot to his revenge, to kill all his father's murderers, then to commit suicide. When it was over, Chris would go back to Kurt, they would get married, Kurt would have a brilliant diplomatic career, his daddy could face the world again, and they'd be rich and happy to the end of their days.

"Chris does her work perfectly, beyond your wildest dreams. And Luçot does everything expected of him. He does his homework in Vienna and Ludwigsburg. At the Zentralstelle he gets all the addresses except Slobodin's. Of course the K.G.B.—and even the C.I.A.—knew where Slobodin was. The Zentralstelle couldn't know because, as far as they were concerned, he was an ex-prisoner-of-war who had remained in Russia. As with the other Russian prisoners, Slobodin had broken all contact with the international organisations serving refugees and former deportees. That is why, when your friends were falsifying the documents at the Zentralstelle, they couldn't insert his address among the others. It would have looked suspicious. So the only way to get Slobodin's address into Luçot's hands was through Christine. The poor girl was made to believe that Kurt Müller's 'Nazi friends' had found it.

"With this behind him, Luçot goes into action. He knocks off Talbot, Brajinski and Dragner. Then comes the really delicate operation: Ponomarev's murder. The timing had to be exact in order to coincide with the few days Ponomarev was to be in New York. The first time I suspected your hand in this was when Chris told me what great pains her 'Nazi friends' had gone to in order to make absolutely sure that Luçot acted on the right date, at the right time. You as much as drove Chris and Luçot to the Plaza and pointed out Ponomarev getting into his car.

"O.K. The murder goes off according to plan. Then Slobodin gets his the next day. Chris and Luçot go back to France and Luçot heads for Israel.

"The moment has come to introduce a new character into the plot. With consummate skill, Hal Richards has convinced the President that Ponomarev was killed by mistake. Now it's time to put a new marionette to work: Jeff Saunders."

Saunders' voice was beginning to grow hoarse. And still no word from Richards.

"Until tonight, Hal, I kept asking myself why you chose me for the job. You'd kicked me out of the service like a dog. I had been one of your best agents. But things began to go sour: I was responsible for the disaster in Czechoslovakia; I'd become a drunk. It was only tonight that I realised why I had the honour of being chosen. You wanted me for two reasons. You knew I'd do anything to win back your confidence and therefore would follow all your instructions to the letter. Secondly, you knew I'd gone to pot and probably wasn't as sharp as I used to be. I wouldn't be able to do anything more than follow the trail you'd marked out for me. You'd scatter the bait and, like a dumb animal, I'd follow it into the trap.

"To be sure, I was a good docile boy at the beginning. I followed the dotted line without a murmur—just like Luçot and Chris before me. I found what you wanted me to find in Miami, in Vienna, in Ludwigsburg, in Paris. What you didn't take into account was the human element: that Christine would have feelings over which you had no control. Mistake number three. In order to detain me, she not only almost killed me, but she took me to my room at the Orly Hilton and we spent the night together. In that short space of time, something happened. I'm not going to go into details, but you might say a kind of bond was established between us. You hadn't thought of that, had you, Hal? That's why she turned to me when I got back from Israel. I'd like to mention in passing that you may have had nothing to do with Jourbin's suicide, but you clearly didn't give a damn whether he lived or died. And that man was innocent, Hal. He had not been involved in Robert Luçot's murder. In fact, he tried to prevent it.

"Well, we'll skip that. While Luçot was in Israel, you moved on to the next phase. The operation was nearing its successful conclusion. The time had come to break with Christine. It was important to get her off-stage before the final curtain because someone might ask her embarrassing questions and she might bring up the whole 'Kurt Müller' episode. But how to do it? Destroy 'Kurt Müller', obviously. That is why you gave Luçot Joakim Müller's address during the one moment he was away from Christine.

"That was the spoke in the wheel. You had overlooked the fact that there was something between Christine and me. In her despair over the collapse of her affair with 'Kurt', she turned to me. Thanks to her, I met Luçot face to face and he told me some things I wasn't supposed to know: Christine's role in the business, the way he got Slobodin and Müller's addresses, and Chris's decision to break with him when she heard the news of Kurt's father's death.

"The rest is simple. When I looked over the documents I'd stolen from the Zentralstelle, I saw right away that Christine couldn't have found Slobodin's address there—as she had told Luçot. A telephone call to Mademoiselle Leroy at the D.S.T. gave me all I needed to know about Chris's father. With that information under my belt, I drove down to see Christine and she filled in the rest.

"You were very displeased with me, Hal. In fact, when you called me in Paris, you were scared stiff. You realised I was about to discover the real story. You knew I was getting too dangerous and that you had to get me back to Washington right away. But it was too late. I didn't give a damn what happened to me, what you thought of me, whether I'd make it back into the service. I wanted only one thing: to know the truth.

"So I telephoned one of my friends at Gehlen—Konrad Von Hase. I'd done him some favours before. I stopped off in Cologne to see him on my way to Vienna. He gave me the answers to the questions I'd asked him by phone from Paris. He confirmed my suspicions that the 'Organisation of Former Internees' in Berne, as well as Monument Verlag Publishers in Munich, were Communist fronts working for the Russians. He also told me that he was certain Joakim Müller had never had a son.

"But I admit that I never would have found the whole truth if I hadn't happened on the original of the Block 13 photograph in Schneider's office. When I saw that Slobodin wasn't in it, it all came clear. That's when I discovered the third truth. All because of that one photograph, Hal. You and your friends didn't know the original was at Schneider's, did you?"

Hal Richards looked at him for a long moment.

"No, Jeff, we did not know about that photograph."

The night wore on, warm and calm. The two men sat opposite each other in silence. Every so often, one or the other got up and refilled the glasses. Then they resumed their studied scrutiny.

"What do you think of my story, Hal?" Saunders asked finally.

"It's a very good story, Jeff. Very interesting."

"Wouldn't a professional say it contained a few errors?"

Hal smiled wearily. "A professional would say it contained very few errors. And he'd add that the story showed a rare intelligence and sharp insight. And the same professional would curse the day he chose you for this mission."

"Do you still intend to drag me to the White House?"

"Of course. Why not? It's going to be a nice, intimate little ceremony. The Secretary of State will be there, and Art Bailey of the F.B.I., and someone from Pentagon intelligence, and two or three generals for window-dressing. Maybe even the Soviet Ambassador. Don't forget you saved the peace of the world. The least we can do is show our gratitude."

"What if I told you I had no intention of coming to your ceremony?"

"That is your privilege, Jeff. I can always find some way of explaining it to the President. And you'll go on lying on your unmade bed with your bottle of whisky to the end of your days—or until the money runs out."

Jeff did not reply.

Richards burst out: "For Christ's sake, say something! Tell me the whole thing was revolting, cruel, cynical. Tell me I'm a bastard. Why don't you say it?"

"I'm not going to say anything of the sort, Hal. It's not for me to judge. You know that. When you choose this profession, you know the kind of thing you're going to be asked to do."

"But you chose this profession too."

"Right. I did."

Richards got to his feet. "Well, say what you like, Jeff. We brought it off! We got rid of Ponomarev, and there's every chance that Gaidukov's nomination will be confirmed. Soviet foreign relations will be in the hands of a man who wants peace. The Russians are happy; America is happy. Anyone who cares about the peace of the world should be satisfied. Sure, some innocent blood was shed. And a girl in love saw her little world collapse. But what's that compared to the danger of nuclear war? How can you compare the loss of seven or eight lives with the destruction of all humanity?"

"That's just what I was saying, Hal. You can't."

Richards looked at him suspiciously.

"You're not planning to resign by any chance?"

"That would be very convenient, wouldn't it, Hal? Well, the answer is no. I'm staying."

"O.K. We'll have plenty of time to see whether your decision is wise. For now, I suggest you take a vacation—two or three months, say. Wherever you like. All expenses paid. I don't want to see you around for the next few weeks; people might start asking questions. Go get a rest until things have calmed down a little. Think of it as a personal service to me."

Saunders gave him a crafty look. "Can you see me going off alone for three months?"

"All right, I get it. Take someone along. I'll pay the chick's expenses too."

Jeff picked up his jacket, drained his glass and headed for the door.

"Just a moment, Jeff! About the White House ceremony ... will you be going?" Richards added dryly: "I hear they break out the booze on these occasions."

"You've convinced me, Hal. I'll be there."

Before going home, Saunders stopped at a bar he knew well and bought a quart of Scotch. He went back to his apartment, sat down on his bed and opened the bottle. Then he picked up the phone and dialled the number for T.W.A. reservations. The ever-charming voice came on.

"I want a ticket to Athens for next Friday."

"Yes, sir. That will be Flight number 702, stopping at Paris and Rome. Departure time from Dulles Airport at seven thirty-five a.m. Arrival time at Athens, eighteen o'clock."

"Fine. Now I'd like you to cable a ticket from Stuttgart to Athens to Fraülein Inge Knutte, Zentralstelle, Ludwigsburg, Germany. At my expense, of course."

The voice repeated the instructions, then added: "For the same day, sir?"

"Yes."

"That will be an Olympic Airways flight. Just one moment please ... Flight 435, leaving Stuttgart at fourteen thirty, arriving Athens, eighteen thirty."

"Perfect."

"Anything else, sir?"

"Yes. I'd like a telex to go with the ticket."

"Yes, sir. What is the message?"

"'How about dinner next Friday?' Signed: 'Jeff Saunders'."

The voice asked for his telephone number and the number of his credit card and hung up. Outside, the first morning light was showing.

186

Sitting numbly by the telephone, Saunders' mind went back to the night Hal Richards had dragged him from this very bed. The events of the past week flicked on and off in his head: Miami Beach. Vienna. The Zentralstelle. Paris. *Letters in Blood.* Dachau. God! Israel and old Jourbin drowned before he could save him. The dead Pole surrounded by a thousand blind eyes. Luçot at his feet. Chris weeping. The two photographs. And all those men, murdered. Then, just now, Richards pontificating: "Say what you like, Jeff, we brought it off!"

Suddenly, he was seized with an attack of nausea. He ran to the bathroom and grasped the washstand with his hands. His entire body contracted. He stood there for a long time, slowly vomiting until his gut was empty. Finally he straightened, washed his face and went back to his room to see if he had a clean shirt for the White House ceremony.

When Saunders had gone, Hal Richards closed the door and walked over to the small safe in the wall behind his desk. With a practised hand, he made the combination, took a bunch of keys from his pocket, found the right one, inserted it in the lock and opened the door.

It contained only one folder. He took it over to a small incinerator standing in a corner, struck a match, regulated the gas and watched the flame as it danced in the oven. He opened the folder and, one by one, fed the sheets into the fire, waiting for each document to be completely consumed before putting in another. By the end of the day, the ashes would be dissolved in a special solution, leaving not a single trace of the documents.

Fifteen minutes later, the job was done. Then he threw in the folder itself and watched it disintegrate in the fire, the flame seeming to hesitate a moment before it attacked the block letters of the title: *Operation Cannibal.* The two words disappeared in a final burst of flame and the powdery remains settled to the bottom of the small crematorium. For a fraction of a second, the C.I.A. chief thought back to other crematoriums in other times.

The ceremony had come to a close. As the President was

seeing his guests to the door, he whispered to Richards: "Could you stay on for a few minutes?"

The two men were finally alone in the Oval Office.

"I am very pleased," the President said. "Very pleased at the way this business was handled. I'm enormously relieved that we were able to avoid a confrontation with the Russians. It was a near thing, you know."

"Yes, Mr. President."

"That man of yours, Saunders ... That was a remarkable piece of work."

"Yes, Mr. President. He is a very clever young man. And may I say, sir, I hope our relations with the Soviet Union continue to improve."

The President frowned. "That's what I wanted to talk to you about, Hal. That was my hope too. But I received this cable this morning from our Ambassador in Moscow ... It's still confidential."

He handed Richards a sheet of white paper with the two diagonal red lines that indicated top secret.

"Read the second paragraph."

Richards read out loud: "A few moments ago, at the close of an all-night meeting, the Presidium of the Supreme Soviet unanimously approved the Politburo's recommendation that Marshal Slavin, Assistant Chief of the General Staff, resign his Army functions and assume the position of Minister of Foreign Affairs, replacing acting-Minister Dimitri Gaidukov who has served in this capacity since the death of Lev Ponomarev.

"What! I don't believe it! Slavin as Foreign Minister? He's worse than Ponomarev! He'll sabotage the Zurich Conference for sure! He'll..."

"Yes, Hal." The President tried to sound calm but his pallor reflected the depth of his anxiety. "But we must adapt ourselves to this new situation. Apparently the solution to Ponomarev's murder came too late. During the past week, the military were able to mount an offensive. They managed to impose their will on the Politburo and force the civilians to agree to Slavin's nomination. They're flexing their muscles—they've tasted power and now they want more. This could be the beginning of a very dangerous period."

188

"What about Gaidukov?"

"Oh, don't worry about him. He'll undoubtedly get his job back as U.N. Ambassador."

"Mr. President, I'm sure you are fully aware of the seriousness of the situation. The Disarmament Conference will be a fiasco. The Russians will be more difficult than ever. I suppose you'll have to go to Congress for additional military aid . . ."

"Yes, I'm afraid that's about it. I wanted you to see the cable, Hal, because I'd like your views on what our options are."

Richards thought for a moment.

"There are three possibilities as I see it, sir. The first is to keep trying for a relaxation of tensions with the Russians—in spite of this set-back. The second is to move much faster in our rapprochement with China . . ."

"And what would be the third possibility?"

"The third possibility . . . Well, I'd like to get some information on Slavin, his past, his habits, his private life and—" He was suddenly silent. "No, Mr. President, I don't think there is a third possibility."

AUTHOR'S NOTE

Although the preceding story is a work of fiction, acts of cannibalism are a part of the sorry history of the concentration camps during World War II. Several incidences were recorded at Dachau and Auschwitz, the largest number occurring among Russian prisoners-of-war at Dachau. Whether the hunger that drove them to these acts was caused by a deliberate policy of starvation or by the Nazis' inability to provide properly for their prisoners has not yet been clearly established.

— Some stilted dialogue.
38/ "I don't want to overdo the dramatic bit".
Ought to have taken your advice.